Feral

A M/M Paranormal Romance

By Alexa Land

**This book contains
sexually explicit material.
It is only intended for adult readers.**

Dedicated to William, with thanks

Table of Contents

Prologue

He was watching me.

I sensed his presence weeks before I saw him. Day after day, I peered out into the woods beside the lake house, unable to shake the feeling that someone was out there. But I never caught a glimpse of him. Eventually, I convinced myself it had to be my imagination, that spending so much time by myself was starting to mess with my mind.

I was so wrong.

Chapter One

"I'm done."

I coughed, struggling to get the big mouthful of fettuccine past the sudden lump in my throat, and finally managed, "Wait, what?"

"I said I'm done," Donnie repeated. "I'm not going to do this anymore." He said it as casually as if he were talking about the weather and took a sip from his glass of wine.

The lump in my throat shifted to the pit of my stomach. "You mean you're breaking up with me?"

"It's time we both moved on." Donnie picked up his fork and knife and dissected the bloody steak on his plate, then popped a piece in his mouth.

I felt like I'd just been kicked in the gut, and completely regretted the heavy meal I'd been packing away just moments before. I stammered, "But why?"

"It's been three years. This thing we've been doing has run its course."

I felt like crying, but fought the tears back with everything I had. "I can't believe you're blind-siding me like this. In public!" We were in one of our favorite restaurants in Belmont Shore. Donnie must have (wrongly) assumed dumping me with an audience would prevent me from making a scene. Yeah, good luck with that.

"Keep your voice down, Nate," he said, his hazel eyes pinning me sharply.

"No! Sorry, I'm not going to keep my voice down!" That got the attention of every person in the swanky little restaurant. "Don't I get a say in this? Aren't we going to talk about it?"

"There's nothing to talk about."

"Like hell there isn't! I mean, come on, how can you—" I was gesturing a bit wildly as I was talking, and suddenly my right hand struck an object that was being carried past our table.

What happened next played out before my eyes almost in slow motion. The shallow dish of flaming cherries jubilee hurtled through the air, landing upside down in Donnie's lap. Never in a million years could I have made that shot intentionally.

In the next instant, the fiery dessert was extinguished by a passing waiter with ninja-like reflexes and a pitcher of iced tea. "Oh God, Donnie, I'm sorry," I stammered.

The worst part of that was the look Donnie gave me as the iced tea dripped off his auburn bangs and soaked into his Armani. It said unmistakably: *I was so right to dump you.*

I was completely mortified, but I simply pushed back from the table and left the restaurant. Miraculously, I didn't trip over anything on the way out.

It was a long walk home to my little apartment near the Long Beach State campus – of course Donnie had driven tonight. And as I walked, I tried to build up some righteous anger. I really didn't want to be sad about getting dumped like that. I wanted to be pissed off.

*****

It had been a Friday night when Donnie dumped me and for the duration of the weekend, I managed to hold on to that anger. I stomped around my apartment, calling him every name in the book (and a few new ones I made up to suit the occasion). I drank far too much Jack Daniels. I made an elaborate funeral pyre of every memento I'd accumulated during my time with him, and set it ablaze in my kitchen sink (this, of course, resulted in needing to beat the smoke alarm to death with a potato masher to get it to shut up again). I only drunk-dialed Donnie twice, and both times I made myself hang up before he answered.

All in all, I felt I was coping quite well. Until 9:18 Monday morning, that is.

I was in my fourth year at Long Beach State and not much closer to a degree than when I'd started. It was far too early on a Monday morning and I was in a huge lecture hall, tired, hung over, and hopelessly lost during Econ.

And that's when I decided to lose it.

Well, okay, I didn't exactly *decide* to lose it then and there. But that's what happened.

I fell apart. Big time. Without warning I started crying, and once the tears started, there was just no stopping them. And it wasn't just crying, but sobbing. And not even just sobbing, but falling-on-the-floor, arms-wrapped-around-myself, making-sounds-like-a-dying-elephant-in-gut-wrenching-agony sobbing.

Okay, I have no idea if elephants actually wail when they die. But I imagine they do, and I imagine it's loud and tormented and completely horrible. I just hope for their sake, they don't have a hundred and fifty undergraduates and one extremely uptight Econ professor staring at them in abject horror while that's going on.

Because that's really no fun.

So anyway, there I was, embarrassing the shit out of myself on the floor in Econ. And at some point, apparently someone called someone, who called someone else, and after a while a couple people showed up and took me to the nurse's office. Then they called my emergency contact.

But my mom wasn't home. Her new husband Irv was.

Irv Azzetti came and picked up my sorry, snot-covered self from school. I had mostly quit sobbing by then, and was in the throes of that gasping hiccup wheeze thing that happens after a really hard crying jag. He took a long look at me and said, "Broken heart, right?" All I could do was nod and gasp-wheeze-hiccup.

He led me with a hand on my shoulder to the parking lot and deposited me in the passenger seat of his flashy silver Cadillac. But he didn't take me home. He took me to a bar instead.

Surprisingly, there was one open for business at ten a.m. on a Monday morning.

"So, kid," he said after we'd each tossed back a couple rounds of whiskey, "not that it's any of my business. But you really shouldn't let some broad fuck you up like this."

Okay, he didn't really say *broad*. He said *girl*. I basically thought of Irv as my own personal Frank Sinatra. He was originally from Hoboken, just like Frank, and twenty years in California had done nothing to curb the accent, the slicked back hair (what there was of it), or the three piece suits. Irv was old-school east coast all the way, and when I looked back on conversations I'd had with him, they were always remembered as being a touch more colorful than was actually the case.

I'd never bothered telling Irv I was gay, because I'd never really had any kind of heart to heart discussion with this man. He'd married Stella, my mom, all of four months ago, and he was her fifth husband, so I hadn't really bothered trying to bond with him. Given Stella's track record, who knew how long he'd be around?

But now I didn't feel like lying to him, so I blurted, "Not a girl. A guy."

To Irv's credit, he took this revelation in stride. All he did was shrug and say, "Well, I suppose a broken heart's a broken heart, no matter who did the breaking."

After a couple more rounds, I started talking. And by that I mean totally spilling my guts. Not just about Donnie, but about everything else that was wrong with my life —

and that was a very long list. I was unemployed for the first time since I was fourteen. My college education was going nowhere slowly. At twenty-two years old, I had absolutely no idea what I wanted to be when I grew up. *If* I ever grew up. I'd drifted away from almost all of my friends from high school, most of which were already out of college with decent jobs. I was a complete and total mess and could clearly see why Donnie had dumped my ass.

Once the flood gates of over-sharing were opened, there was no stopping me. I'm not really sure how long I went on like that, detailing every single thing that was wrong in my life to a virtual stranger. But Irv was a great listener. He didn't interrupt, except to ask an occasional question. And when I finally ran out of steam, he simply said, "You know what you need, Nate? Some time to figure out who you are and what you want."

"Well yeah, but—"

Now he interrupted me. "The broken heart, that'll heal on its own. Just give it a few weeks. But you got a lot of bigger issues you need to address, a lot of things you need to work out for yourself. Let me ask you this: what do you like doing?"

I thought about it for a while as I pushed my shaggy light brown hair out of my green eyes, then ventured, "I dunno. I guess I like writing."

"Yeah? You any good?"

I shrugged and looked down at the scarred tabletop. "I don't know."

"Stella says you're good. She says that English was your best subject in high school."

I just shrugged again.

"When was the last time you wrote anything, besides a paper for school?"

"I guess it's been years."

"What I think you need is a chance to be by yourself for a while. You need some time to dig deep. Discover what makes you tick. Maybe write a little, see if that still grabs you." He grinned widely. "And I know just where you need to go to get some answers."

Irv had been fifty eight when he met my mom, and a lifelong bachelor. Stella was a package deal: when he'd married her, he abruptly became the stepdad of five boys. He didn't know a damn thing about kids, so he'd gone for the obvious shortcut: buying their affection.

My three youngest brothers were pushovers: an Xbox and a stack of video games, and they were a done deal. My seventeen year old brother Patrick was also no challenge. He got a six year old Honda Civic, and after that, Irv was his new BFF.

The path to my affection hadn't been quite so obvious. Not that I wanted anything from him. I liked this guy, and was glad that he made my mom happy. But my brothers had received gifts, and Irv had been determined that I shouldn't be left out. And now apparently he'd finally figured out what to do for me, and was clearly delighted at the prospect.

Chapter Two

So that was the series of events that led to me packing up my possessions, surrendering my security deposit to my roommates, dropping that semester's classes, and heading to Del Norte County in northernmost California.

Irv owned a lake house up there, one he'd inherited from a favorite aunt about twenty years ago, and he was letting me use it for free through the end of summer. He said this was the perfect place for me to 'find myself.' Since the prospect of time alone had sounded absolutely wonderful, I hadn't argued.

He'd warned me that the location was remote. I kept expecting creepy banjo music as my twenty-six-year-old Jeep bucked and lunged over the seventeen miles of deeply rutted dirt road that led to the house. I was sure once I got there I'd find a tumble-down log cabin with a family of rabid raccoons holed up in the kitchen cabinets.

So when I finally rounded the last bend of the dirt road from hell, I was in for a surprise. Before me stood a mid-century modern home, elegant and impressive in a wide clearing on the banks of a pretty sapphire lake. What a relief!

I came to a stop in the shade of a big redwood, and took in my surroundings. Besides the house, there were two outbuildings off to the far left, one of which was apparently a garage with a big propane tank tucked behind it, the other some kind of storage shed.

From here, none of it looked like rabid raccoon headquarters. I was cautiously optimistic as I grabbed the envelope Irv had given me, dumped out the key, and swung my stiff legs out of the Jeep.

The front door was around the side and to the rear of the building, and I quickly saw why it had been positioned there. The house appeared to be made almost entirely of glass. With the exception of the back of the house and a wrap-around eight-foot wide wall bracketing both sides of the building, the rest was all windows. This showcased a gorgeous view of the sparkling little lake, and the meadow and thick pine forest to either side of the house.

The windows also showcased *me*, I noted as I stepped into the living room and glanced up at the two-story high glass walls. The fishbowl sensation was impossible to miss. I was glad the nearest neighbors were more than twenty miles away.

I wandered into the kitchen, flipping on a light switch since the sun was beginning to set outside, and tossed my keys on the counter. Irv told me his housekeeper had come in to tidy up the place and fill the pantry, after I'd agreed that spending some time here sounded like a good idea. This person normally came in a couple times a year to air the place out and knock down the cobwebs.

There was a note from the housekeeper on the counter, in such tiny, disheveled handwriting that it was all I could do to make out the words. His name was Chuck, or Chet (I could barely read the signature), and he'd provided his phone number in case of emergency, but pointed out that I'd have to drive at least fifteen miles back toward town before I could actually expect any cell phone reception. Judging by the shakiness of his handwriting, I imagined Chuck/Chet to be about a hundred and fifty years old.

I took a look in the huge refrigerator, and found that the housekeeper had been quite ambitious in stocking it. It was packed to the point of exploding. I grabbed a beer and headed out to the deck behind the house, then sank down onto a comfortable padded lounge chair and let my eyes slide shut.

The drive from Long Beach had left me beyond exhausted. It had taken the better part of two days (with last night spent in some anonymous roadside motel) and that last section, the dirt road, had taken an eternity. It was a damn good thing I drove a Jeep, although when I'd bought it second-hand, the purchase had been all about vanity and not practicality. It's not like anyone actually needed a four-by-four in southern California.

*****

Apparently, I fell asleep out there on the deck.

I woke with a start, disoriented in the darkness. The only illumination came through the windows from the single light fixture I'd left on in the kitchen. And thank God that was on, because it would have been pitch black otherwise.

There had been a loud, sharp sound, something barely remembered now, that had awakened me. I strained to listen, but all I heard was a steady chorus of frogs and crickets. I sat up quickly, knocking over the beer when I swung my legs to one side of the lounge chair. It was still unopened and rolled off the edge of the deck.

Though it was mid-April, it was absolutely freezing. My thin t-shirt and jeans were useless against the cold and I wrapped my arms around myself, my breath forming a cloud as I stumbled inside. I was shivering violently as I pulled the door shut behind me and hurried up the stairs.

The top floor of the house was all one huge bedroom, an open loft overlooking the living room below. I went straight through to the bathroom, turning on the shower and stripping quickly as I gritted my teeth to keep them from knocking together. The hot water was such a shock against my cold skin that I yelped as I got in. I held my face up to the water, then let it run over the top of my head, matting down my hair, pushing it into my eyes. And I wondered as I stood under the spray if I would have actually frozen to death, had I remained out on that deck all night.

After maybe twenty minutes in the shower my body temperature had returned to normal, so I shut off the water and wrapped myself in a big towel. The house was incredibly cold, and the clothes I'd been wearing were now a soggy mess on the bathroom floor because I hadn't noticed a gap in the shower curtain. Awesome. As was the fact that the rest of my clothes were still in the car. I really didn't want to go back out into the dark, frigid night to retrieve my luggage.

In the bedroom, I pulled the blanket off the odd, huge bed and wrapped myself up in it. The bed stood in the very center of the room, its headboard an artistic wrought iron representation of leafless trees, iron branches intertwining gracefully left to right. The footboard was similar, but much lower so as not to block what would probably be an incredible view of the lake when it was light out. The bed and dark red duvet didn't match anything else in the house, which was all pale Scandinavian wood and soft shades of sand. But here, apparently, Irv's Aunt Rose had allowed herself a bit of romantic license.

I searched the walls for a thermostat, then headed downstairs, the heavy duvet trailing behind me. The kitchen was nestled underneath the loft bedroom, open to the rest of the downstairs, and there I found the thermostat and turned the little dial as high as it would go. I grabbed a box of crackers from the cabinet and perched on a little stool at the breakfast bar, and wondered if the heater actually worked as I tore open the package.

Soon I had my answer, as twenty years' worth of dust began to burn off the heating elements. The smell was truly awful, and my eyes watered as I coughed and rushed to the front door, sticking my head out into the cold night and drawing in big lungfuls of fresh air. I wondered if the dust might actually cause a fire, and left the door open as I rushed back to the thermostat and shut it off. Freezing was better than burning down Irv's beloved lake house on my first day here.

I sat in the open doorway as the choking fumes slowly lessened and pulled the blanket tightly around my body. Soon I was shivering violently again. I did warm up a bit when a moth of monster movie proportions flew in through the open door and I had to run around after it, naked and yelling and waving my arms, surely looking like a complete and total lunatic. Eventually I managed to get Mothra back outside, herding it through the door with a copy of Sunset magazine from the mid-1980s. But as soon as I settled down again, the cold descended.

I needed my clothes, not that I relished the idea of going out in the cold, dark night. I grabbed my car keys and peered out the glass door. The light from the house spilled out about twenty feet into the night, illuminating a bit of the meadow but leaving the forest beyond it pitch black. Kinda creepy.

Okay, best to just get this over with. I left the blanket behind since dragging it through the dirt seemed like a bad idea, and threw the door open and rushed out into the bitter cold, cursing vividly all the way to my car. Doing this naked was silly, but doing it without shoes was downright dumb. A million stones and pine needles and God knows what else cut into the soles of my feet.

I unlocked my Jeep and pulled down the zipper of my big blue duffle bag, then fished around in it for my flip flops, my teeth chattering. I put them on quickly, and then pulled on my cotton hoodie before shouldering the heavy bag and grabbing my backpack. Oh yeah, this was an awesome look: flip flops and a jacket with no pants.

A faint rustling sound in the woods behind me made the skin on the back of my neck prickle. I whirled around, peering into the darkness, and wondered if there were bears in this part of California. I decided not to stick around and find out.

I ran back inside and locked the door behind me, then dressed quickly. After that I turned my attention to the big double-sided stone fireplace, free-standing near the center of the living room. I'd never tried to build a fire before. It wasn't like the shabby two bedroom apartment my mom and brothers and I had shared for much of my childhood had come with a fireplace. Neither did the even shabbier apartment I'd moved into with three roommates when I left home. And it wasn't like my dad, who'd left when I was three, or any of the men Stella married and divorced after him, had ever taken me camping and taught me to build a campfire or anything.

But I thought, how hard could it be?

The answer to that question came about half an hour later, when my every effort at getting a fire going produced not so much as a smolder. The wood I'd piled into the hearth wasn't even slightly singed and I was rapidly running out of matches.

I was off to a gloriously pathetic start here in Del Norte County.

I wrapped myself in the big red blanket and stretched out on the floor beside the fireplace, staring up at the high ceiling. Why did I think I could do this? Why did I think I could do *anything*? Donnie had been right to leave me. I was a complete disaster. It was a wonder that he'd even stuck around for three years.

Well, then again, I could see why he'd stuck around. Most of our time together had been spent in bed, after all, where I'd been all too willing to give him whatever he wanted.

I'd been a nineteen-year-old virgin when we met. Donnie was twenty-six at the time, a handsome lawyer with thick auburn hair and perfect clothes and a perfect smile. He picked me up in a grocery store, and took me home and taught me how to suck his cock. What I lacked in experience I must have made up for in sheer enthusiasm, because he kept calling after that. Once or twice a week, he'd take me out to dinner, then back to his house – or, more specifically, his bed. Occasionally, he'd skip the dinner part and cut straight to fucking me.

Before Donnie, I thought I'd never find a boyfriend. All through high school, I was shy and awkward and totally in the closet. I was also completely naïve, and had no clue how two guys let each other know they were interested. I remember wondering if I was the only gay person at my huge school. Which, okay, was statistically impossible, but no one was obviously out among the rest of the student population.

Then Donnie came along partway through my freshman year of college. He'd been perfectly straightforward about what he wanted, and I was amazed that what he wanted was me. We dated for three years, and you know how that ended. And yeah, okay, I get that what we were doing wasn't really a relationship by most definitions. It was primarily just sex – at least to him. But to me it had meant so much more than that.

I never asked for more or expected better. I never did anything to rock the boat. I was sure he'd dump me the moment I did anything besides get on my knees for him, so I kept quiet.

And he dumped me anyway.

Chapter Three

I couldn't help but notice that I'd failed to freeze to death.

My back was to the fireplace, so the first thing I saw when I awoke was the lake, sparkling in the early morning light. The blanket slid from my shoulders and pooled in my lap as I sat up and stretched my arms over my head.

I realized that this house had a huge design flaw: with almost no interior walls, save for the ones framing the bathroom, and no means of blocking off the massive windows, you really had no choice but to wake up with the sun each day. Not my idea of a good time.

The blanket dropped to the floor as I got to my feet and stretched my back. It was pleasantly warm in here for some reason. A crackling sound behind me made me jump, and I spun around to find the fire burning brightly, warming the entire room. But how? I'd tried so hard to light it and I'd failed miserably.

As if an answer might present itself in the flames, I knit my brows and stared at the fire for a while. Maybe some little ember had ignited after all in my dozens of attempts at getting a fire going. There really was no other explanation.

I made myself a pot of coffee and took a cup out to the deck and stared out at the water. It was freezing out here, but the cold was helping wake me up so I didn't mind it. I wondered idly if the lake had a name. Irv hadn't mentioned it. He'd also told me very little about his Aunt Rose, and as I glanced around me, I wondered about the woman who had built such a grand house in the middle of fuck-all nowhere. And it hadn't been a vacation home for her, she'd lived here year-round.

Didn't the isolation get to her? I wondered if it would get to me. But as a true introvert, I was guessing it would be awhile before I started to miss human interaction. I'd brought a huge box of books along that would probably sufficiently keep me company, stuff I'd been collecting for years but hadn't made the time for between work and school and Donnie.

Shit. And now I was thinking about him again.

Tears prickled at the back of my eyes, but I was done crying over this. I didn't want to keep being so hurt and sad and miserable. Impulsively, I let out a yell, and it felt pretty good. So I kept yelling, purging myself of some of that hurt, that anger. The noise echoed out over the water. It went on for a while – I had a lot to let out.

Yelling was surprisingly exhausting, and I ended up laying on the rough redwood boards of the deck after that, panting, feeling as drained as if I'd just run twenty miles. I rolled onto my back and stared up at the cloudless sky. My head felt like it was going to split open from the exertion of yelling, and my throat felt like I'd swallowed glass. Despite that though, I actually felt a little better, calmer somehow.

Irv had been right to send me someplace isolated. I wondered if he'd somehow anticipated my need to yell until my voice gave out, something I could never do in the middle of the city. Maybe he'd known how much that would help.

Okay, I thought to myself, *let's call that the Nathaniel Logan Recovery Plan, Phase One: yelling your damn lungs out.* Now I just had to figure out what the hell Phase Two was.

Chapter Four

Over the next week, I settled into a comfortable routine at the lake house. I no longer thought of Donnie every five minutes...though I did think about him a lot. I learned to make a fire in the big stone fireplace and felt caveman proud at that accomplishment. I gradually, in tiny increments, burned all the dust off the central heating system while keeping all the doors and windows open. I read four books before realizing I needed to pace myself or risk burning through my entire supply before even a month was out. And I began running every day, pushing myself harder and farther than I ever had before.

I'd been a runner since my early teens, always loving the way it cleared my mind and quieted me. I'd been pretty decent on my high school track team, not a star, but certainly holding my own. I was a distance runner despite my coach's misguided efforts to make me into a sprinter, and out here in the woods I could really apply myself to this pursuit.

Every day, I ran along the reasonably level edge of the rutted dirt road leading back to town, since there was no alternative route that I could see. One day, I drove the seventeen miles back along that dirt road, marking each mile with a bit of twine tied to a tree branch, so I could gauge my progress.

At about the twelve mile mark I got cell phone reception, but just barely. I got out of my car, holding my cell phone out in front of me like a divining rod, trying to get a second bar to go with the flickering first I'd picked up. I ended up climbing onto the hood of my Jeep, which inexplicably netted me three bars, and placed a call to Irv at his office. I got his voice mail.

"Hey Irv, it's Nate. Just wanted to check in, let you know I got to the lake house last Friday and all is well. There's no cell phone reception at the house, but you probably know that, so I can only check in when I head to town. Coming here was a great suggestion. I'm thinking I will stay through the end of summer, like you said."

I shifted the phone to the other ear and added, "I'm doing a lot better, by the way. I know what a mess I was that Monday when you picked me up from school. Thank you again for that, for coming to get me, then listening while I spilled my guts, and you know, not judging. Okay, I better go. Please say hi to Mom and Ryan and the other kids for me. I—" the shrill beep announcing the end of the recording cut me off.

I tried calling their condo next. Again I got voice mail and left a quick message for my little brother. Ryan was six, and the greatest little kid in the history of great little kids. I was going to miss him like crazy this summer. I adjusted the friendship bracelets he'd made for me, faded strips of woven thread that were tied permanently to each of my wrists.

And then for a few stupid moments, I considered calling Donnie. *Just to say hi*, I lied to myself. Secretly, I hoped he missed me and regretted our break-up. But then I decided I was being pathetic, and hopped down off the hood of my car.

When I got back to the house, I still had the whole day stretching before me. That was the problem with getting up at dawn (as I had every day I'd been here, thanks to the wall o' windows) – the days were just *so long*.

After lunch, I headed out to the deck with one of my lined notebooks and tried to write, but soon gave up and picked up a book instead. The weather was perfect, the sun warming my skin, so I decided to sunbathe while I read. I glanced at my surroundings – the meadow that bridged the space from the house to the forest's edge, the lake, and back behind me to the dirt road. What the hell did I think I was looking for? This place was beyond isolated.

I stripped myself completely naked. When else would I ever have the opportunity for an all-over tan? It turned out that being outside like this gave me an odd little thrill, and my cock stirred to life. It had been a few days since I'd found release, my libido having taken a hiatus in the wake of Donnie dumping me. But now I spit in my palm and began to stroke myself. And in just a few minutes I was cumming in huge bursts across my stomach, my chest, even onto my face as I cried out. Yeah, it really had been a while.

Apparently my yell startled a small herd of deer, who startled me in return as they darted out of the forest to my far right. Their hooves tore up the pebbled shore at the edge of the lake as they bolted past me, crossing in front of the deck before finally diving back into the forest off to the left. I shook my head at animals stupid enough to run *toward* a loud noise, instead of away from it.

I fell back onto the lounge chair, trying to catch my breath, my left hand resting on my cock. I was a gross, sticky mess – that had been *a lot* of cum. I grabbed my t-shirt and used it to wipe myself off, then tossed the soiled t-shirt on top of the pile of my clothes on the deck.

As soon as my breathing and heart rate returned to normal, I got up and headed for the shower. Just as I reached the door, a sharp cracking sound like wood splintering made me whirl around. My breath caught in my throat, my heart pounding as the hairs on the back of my neck stood up. I scanned the forest, but saw nothing.

After a few moments, I exhaled and made myself relax. Branches fell off trees all the time, right? Trees fell over, too. *If a tree falls in the woods, and only a naked, cum-soaked boy is there to hear it...* I thought with a little grin, and went to take my shower.

Chapter Five

A lovely Jack Daniels hangover was waiting for me the next morning, thanks to the stash I'd had the foresight to bring with me from Long Beach. I hadn't really set out to get drunk last night, but regardless of my intentions, that had been the end result. This would have been an excellent morning not to wake up with the sun. But sleeping in was just never going to happen in this house, thanks to the genius of Frank Lloyd Wrong – the fictitious designer to whom I'd assigned responsibility for this place.

I went downstairs, dragging the big red blanket with me like a hermit crab's shell, and fired up the coffee machine. Then I folded myself up until I was resting my pounding forehead against the cool stone kitchen counter, and stayed in this position until the coffee was ready.

A search through the cabinets found only dainty little coffee mugs, and they just weren't going to cut it this morning. So I located a straw and launched it into the coffee pot, then brought the pot with me. I grabbed my sunglasses from the counter, shoved them into place, and headed to the deck.

I sank onto the lounge chair and took a long drink of coffee through the straw. The caffeine, coupled with being outside, made me feel a bit better. I loved this deck and had taken to spending most of my time out here, making up for a lifetime without so much as a balcony, let alone a backyard.

It would have been easy to fall back asleep out here, and as I cocooned myself in the puffy blanket, my mind started to drift. And then, inexplicably, the skin on the back of my neck prickled. I sat up quickly, whipping my head around to the right. I had the eerie sensation of being watched, certainly not for the first time since I'd been here, and scanned the forest.

But of course no one was there.

I rolled my eyes at myself and settled back down with my coffee, contemplating the day ahead of me. I'd been wholly unproductive since I'd been here. And I was apparently supposed to be figuring out my life somehow. I wondered if I was expected to have actual answers when I returned to civilization in a few months.

The thought of going home at some point was sort of jarring, since I didn't actually have a home these days. I'd given up my miserable little apartment near the Long Beach State campus, and it wasn't like I had enough money for first, last, and deposit on a new place. So I supposed I'd be moving in with my mom and her new husband and my brothers when I finally left here. It was a big step backward to move in with my family, and lord knew I'd done precious little moving forward in my life. But I really didn't see any alternatives. I sighed, feeling deflated now, and scooped up the blanket and went back inside.

I took some Advil and stood under a hot shower, then dressed quickly and started cleaning up. My time here was clearly not meant to be spent getting drunk, jerking off, and pretty much trashing the house, and I was feeling guilty. And also highly over-caffeinated.

I gathered an armload of towels and clothes, and deposited them in the antiquated but still quite functional laundry room out in the detached garage. Then I jogged to the deck and gathered up my shorts, underwear, and socks from yesterday. But where was my t-shirt? It was one of my favorites, pale blue with the word *Nirvana* so faded out it was almost illegible. I looked left and right, wondering if the shirt had blown off the deck.

I walked to the water's edge and peered into the greenish depths, in case it had blown in this direction. But there was no sign of it. Then I wondered, remembering what I'd last used it for, if some kind of animal had come along and dragged it off, attracted by the…um…protein. I wrinkled my nose and gave my t-shirt up for lost as I went back inside.

Dishes were next, followed by some overall cleaning. There. I felt less guilty now.

The next order of business was more difficult than tidying up the place. I was actually going to try to write something today. I automatically went to the deck, notebook in hand and pen stuck behind my ear. It was again turning into a fairly warm day, so I peeled off my t-shirt, then stared at the blank page for a really long time, tapping the cheap ballpoint pen against the spiral binding.

Eventually I began to doodle. This was pretty much what had gotten me through grade school, high school, and college. I smirked and thought maybe that explained why I wasn't even close to a degree after four years. At first it was just random shapes, patterns, lines, squiggles. But as my imagination engaged, I got more creative. I drew a flipbook in the bottom right corner: a bear lumbering out of the forest, putting on my Nirvana t-shirt, then playing air guitar before he wandered off. It looked like a kid had drawn it, but it made me smile.

I drew for hours, finally stopping when my left hand was completely cramped and smeared all along its outer edge with blue ink. I went inside and ate some lunch, then decided to look for some pencils. I began to search in the kitchen drawers, feeling a bit like I was intruding on Aunt Rose's personal space. Which I supposed was a bit daft, since she'd been dead for twenty years.

Finally, in a junk drawer I found some yellow number two pencils and something else: an old-fashioned brass key on a long, pale blue silk ribbon. I always thought of this type of object as a skeleton key, though I didn't know if that term was meant to refer to something specific. This was over four inches long, an elaborate base of stamped metal giving way to a slender, cylindrical neck, ending in a pair of intricate metal teeth. It was absolutely beautiful. I wondered what it could possibly open in this 1960's-era house. Probably nothing. Maybe Aunt Rose had just found it at an antique sale or something, maybe it had spoken to her the same way it was speaking to me now. I left it out on the counter.

Then I grabbed the pencils and headed back to the deck. I adjusted the lounge chair so it was flat, then flopped down on my stomach and opened the notebook to a blank page. It really was developing into quite a warm day, and the sun felt wonderful on my back. After a minute I grinned and jumped up and kicked off my flip flops, then shucked off my shorts and boxers and returned to my previous position. I hadn't gotten very far yesterday on my all-over tan.

I ended up spending the whole day outside, doodles and cartoons evolving into actual sketching. I'd always loved to draw, but always wished I was better at it. My skill level really didn't matter right now, though.

After a while, I picked up one of the padded wooden chairs that bracketed a small, round table and carried it off the deck, my pencil clutched between my teeth. I waded barefoot through the field, then plunked the chair down amid the tall grasses. I tucked my feet under me, rotated my lined notebook so it was horizontal, and began to sketch the house. My first attempt was too quick and rough. I turned the page and tried again, taking my time.

When I finally came out of my reverie, it was close to sunset. It had cooled down a lot, and I sat in the shadow of the nearby forest, still completely naked. I hadn't even noticed I'd gotten goose bumps, that's how focused I'd been on my sketches.

I stood and stretched. I was hungry, and stiff from having remained seated for so long. But I was something else, too.

I was happy.

I wasn't sure why I felt this good, but I just went with it. I jogged across the field with my pencil and notebook, and bounded onto the deck. My clothes were laying in the fading sunlight, pleasantly warm to the touch, and I pulled them on.

Once back inside, I dug through my duffle bag, eventually unearthing my cheap MP3 player and the little speaker I had to go with it, and brought both to the kitchen with me, filling the house with music for the first time since I'd been here.

At some point in the last couple years, I'd discovered grunge. From the first time I heard Kurt Cobain's voice I'd been hopelessly hooked, not just on Nirvana, but on everything from that era. Now I cranked the little speaker as loud as it would go without disintegrating into static, Eddie Vedder declaring, "I'm still alive." I sang along, loudly and badly as I made dinner. Nirvana's 'All Apologies' was next. I yelled along with the lyric, "Everyone is gay," then air guitared my heart out. Not that this was an air guitar kind of song, but still.

I settled down enough to finish making and eating dinner as songs from two decades past kept me company, and afterwards I went in search of some drawing paper. There was a little desk to one side of the big bedroom, and I sat in the dainty chair and pulled open the drawers one by one. A cool antique typewriter was nestled in the bottom drawer, and I pulled it out and ran a fingertip lightly over the keys. I decided to leave it on the desk.

The typewriter had been sitting on a pale green cardboard box, which contained a big stack of typing paper. The paper was slightly yellowed around the edges, but still perfectly good. "Thank you, Aunt Rose," I murmured. Irv had insisted I help myself to whatever I wanted around the house, which for the most part I avoided. It made me feel weird somehow, even if Aunt Rose was no longer among the living. But I made an exception for this paper, which I was guessing hadn't mattered a whole lot to her.

I went to close the drawer that had housed the typewriter, but something caught my eye. A tan cardboard folder was all that remained at the bottom of the drawer. I lifted it out and folded back the cover. And stopped breathing.

I was staring into the face of the most beautiful person I'd ever seen.

The black and white portrait was of a man in maybe his late twenties. His pale skin was flawless, unlined, suggesting he was young when this picture was taken. But his eyes held a kind of wisdom, which made me place his age a bit higher than I would have otherwise.

His features were classically handsome, almost aristocratic: high cheekbones, a straight nose, full lips. His thick black hair hung past the white collar of his shirt, almost touching his dark suit jacket, and was slicked into a wave that fell across his forehead. Captivating pale eyes, offset by thick, dark lashes, stared directly at the camera.

He was perfection.

"Oh my God," I murmured, and exhaled slowly.

Carefully, I slid the photo from its little cardboard folder and turned it over. On the back, in feminine handwriting, were just these words: Nikolai, 1927.

"Nikolai." The name was as beautiful as he was. Romantic somehow, too.

I couldn't put the photo down. I couldn't stop staring at it. It's difficult to explain my reaction. On the surface there was, of course, raw physical attraction. My heart raced just from the sight of him. But there was more than that at work.

I felt a surge of emotions in looking at this man, this stranger who'd lived decades before I'd been born. Among them was a profound sense of loss – which was, of course, ridiculous. He'd never been mine to lose, existing so far from me in time that I was mourning an impossibility.

And yet, a dull, hollow ache filled me. A longing. A need. I ran my fingertip along the curve of his jaw. The photo had been taken over eighty five years ago. He wouldn't still be alive. He couldn't be. He'd been, and he'd gone, and I never knew him.

With that misplaced longing still washing over me, I eventually slid the photo back into its sleeve and made myself fold the cardboard cover closed again. But I didn't return the picture to its drawer. Instead, I carried it across the room and put it in the nightstand.

Closer to me.

Chapter Six

Two weeks into my stay at the lake house, I had my first visitors. The housekeeper arrived, driven by his great grandson. And it turned out his name was neither Chuck, nor Chet. It was Chad. And Chad was, in fact, older than God.

He was at least eighty, a tiny little man with thin white hair, a big nose, and a quick smile. I'd never felt particularly tall at five foot ten, but he was so short that he made me feel like Chewbacca to his Yoda.

His great grandson Bill was probably in his early forties. When I found myself alone with Bill in the kitchen shortly after their arrival, I just had to ask, "Why on earth is Chad still working?"

Bill looked amused as he said, "You wanna try telling him to retire?"

"He doesn't have to come out to the house while I'm here," I said. "I can drive into town myself for groceries, and I'm already keeping up on the housework. The thought of him cleaning up after me makes me feel guilty as hell."

"Don't worry, I do all the labor-intensive stuff for him. And Grandpop likes coming here.

He and Rose Azzetti were thick as thieves and that's the reason he's stuck with this job even at his age, out of loyalty to her. Plus," Bill added, "Your stepdad Irv pays him a small fortune for what's usually a twice-yearly gig."

"Irv's incredibly generous."

"That he is."

After a moment, I asked embarrassedly, "So, were Chad and Rose...involved?"

Bill grinned at that. "Nah. They were just good friends. Grandpop's been married for over fifty years and he's as faithful as they come."

Chad bustled into the kitchen, carrying a bag of groceries and saying, "A healthy lad like you has probably eaten through most of the refrigerator by now, so this ought to keep you going a bit longer." His voice was clear and strong, so that if you didn't look at who was talking, you'd expect it to be a man half his age.

"Thank you so much, Chad," I said, taking the bag from him. He and I both began transferring groceries to the refrigerator.

"I'll see what's left out in the SUV," Bill said as he exited the kitchen.

When the food was put away, I held up the skeleton key that was still on the counter. "Do you happen to know what this goes to?"

Chad glanced at it and said, "Of course. That opens Rose's art studio."

"Art studio? Where is that?"

He inclined his head and said, "Out past the garage. Must be a frightful mess by now, too. That was Rose's sacred space, she never let me and my broom in there."

I had no idea what building he was referring to. There wasn't anything beyond the garage that I'd ever seen, unless it was set back into the woods a bit. I asked hesitantly, "Do you think it'd be okay if I took a look at it some time?"

"Why wouldn't it be?"

"I don't know. Maybe it would it be disrespectful."

That earned me a smile. "She only told me *I* had to leave it alone. She never said *you* had to."

I grinned at that. "I wish I'd known Rose." I kind of felt like I did, living here in her home with all her things.

"You'd have liked her," he told me. "Everyone did. She was a hell of a gal."

"Why do you think she never married?" I asked, gradually leading up to my real question.

"People asked her that all the time. She always told 'em she'd been in love once, and one heartbreak was enough for this lifetime."

"The man she was in love with…was his name Nikolai?"

"That's right. Why? Did you find some mention of that name around here?"

"Yeah, and I was kind of curious about him." I tried to sound casual when I asked, "Did you ever meet him?"

"Nope. I started working for Rose in 1960. Whatever happened between her and that man was in the distant past by then."

"Did she ever mention his last name?"

"Not that I recall."

Chad was looking at me closely. I'd tried to be nonchalant as I asked these questions, but my face or my voice must have given something away. I only hoped that he couldn't somehow sense the obsession that had gripped me over the last few days.

After finding Nikolai's photo, I'd tried my best to put it out of my mind. That had lasted about an hour. After that, I'd meticulously searched every square inch of this house, every cabinet, box, drawer, envelope and slip of paper. I'd searched the garage, then located the keys to the storage shed and searched there, too.

I had hoped to find a snippet of information on the man in that photo. Anything. But there had been nothing to find.

I ducked my head and busied myself by wiping down the counter. It was bad enough that I thought I was going nuts with this obsession. Best not to make others think so, too.

After a flurry of activity that lasted about an hour, Bill told me as I walked him out to his SUV, "We'll be back two weeks from today."

"Thanks. You really don't have to, though."

Bill flashed me a smile. "Your stepdad's paying us a hefty bonus to come out here every couple weeks and check on you. He's worried about you all alone up here, worried that maybe you'll get sick or injured and not have any way of getting help." That was kind of surprising. Irv barely knew me. "So, is there anything specific you'd like us to bring you when we come back?"

"Oh…no. Irv's already been so generous with the house and the groceries and everything. I don't want to spend any more of his money." I studied my worn out Converse.

Bill regarded me for a long moment, and then he clapped me on the shoulder. It startled me, and I quickly met his gaze. He was beaming at me. "You're all right Nate, you know that? I like that you're not trying to take advantage of Irv. A guy like him, well, it seems like there are always people willing to exploit his generosity."

"I'd never do anything like that."

"I know. So, seriously, what can we bring you when we come back? Surely there's something you want, and Irv really won't mind. As it is, we're only spending a small portion of the budget he set aside for you."

After a moment's hesitation I admitted, "Well, if it's not a lot of trouble, I'd like some art supplies."

"Art supplies?" Bill echoed.

"Yeah. Just, like, some paper and pencils. Oh, and a little portable pencil sharpener. The one Rose had broke, so I've been using a pocket knife to keep my pencils sharp and it's kind of a pain." I looked up at him. "Is that okay? I mean, I saw the little town up the road when I came here, and there's not much by way of shopping. I can't imagine where you'd get stuff like that around here, and I don't know how expensive it would be."

"That's it? That's all you want, some paper and pencils? And you were worried about asking for that?"

"And a sharpener, please."

He was smiling again. "That really won't be a problem, Nate." Great, he probably thought I was an idiot now.

"Please don't go out of your way, though. If it's hard to get, I don't need anything."

"It's no problem at all. We'll be running up to the Fred Meyer in Brookings for your groceries, that's near where we live. They'll have what you need."

"Okay. Thank you."

Soon Bill and his great granddad took off, leaving me alone once again. It had been nice having people to talk to, but the quiet felt good, too. I went around to the deck and picked up the paperback I'd dropped when the sound of their SUV had startled me and sank onto the lounge chair.

The back of my neck prickled like it often did as I sat there. The feeling of being watched was so common now that I didn't even glance over to my right anymore, looking for faces in the forest that just weren't there. I figured it must be a symptom of so much time spent alone, a slight paranoia borne out of isolation.

I couldn't concentrate on the pages of the book, and soon set it aside. I was dying to go check out that art studio. I was hoping against hope that I might find some information in there about Nikolai. About a person who must have died decades ago. A stranger in a photograph.

The man who haunted my dreams every night.

My dreams of Nikolai began the day I found the photograph. They were incredibly vivid, sometimes almost indistinguishable from reality. Some of the dreams were deeply sexual – Nikolai fucking me, or me fucking him, both of us crying out together, shaking with need and pleasure in each other's arms. I usually woke from those dreams covered in sweat and yelling his name.

But not all the dreams were about sex. In some he was in bed with me, holding me gently in the dark, talking to me quietly, soothingly. I could never quite remember later what we'd been talking about.

Those dreams were even harder to cope with than the sexual ones. I'd wake up cold and alone in bed in the middle of the night, again saying his name in the dark stillness of the lake house. On those nights, the nights when I dreamt of myself in his arms and then woke up without him, I felt more alone than I ever had in my entire lonely life.

And yes, I was sure I was completely losing my mind. I fully realized the insanity of dreaming about and obsessing over a face in a photograph. Over a man I never knew, and could never know.

I made token attempts at fighting my descent into total bat-shit craziness. That's what I was doing now: trying to be sane, trying not to run off blindly into the woods chasing ghosts, looking for that art studio just in case it might contain a snippet of information about Nikolai.

It was a battle I was absolutely going to lose.

After not even ten minutes I leapt from the lounge chair, launched myself off the deck and dashed into the house, snatching the key off the kitchen counter. Then I was back outside, running over to the two outbuildings. *Out past the garage.* That was all Chad had said. Why hadn't I asked for more information? 'Out past the garage' was a thick pine forest, and if there had ever been any paths leading into it, they were long since grown over.

I began to pick my way carefully into the forest, fully aware that I had a lousy sense of direction and that it would be all too easy to get lost out in these woods. I tried to go in a straight line, keeping the lake to my right. After a few minutes, I began to think I had to have passed it. And then suddenly, a large clearing appeared up ahead.

Stepping out from the thick, shaded canopy of the forest, I surveyed the meadow before me. It was bright and cheerful, white and yellow wildflowers clustered with bright shocks of orange California poppies. The meadow would have looked completely untouched by civilization, except for the tumbledown chimney rising from one end of it.

I pushed my way through the tall grasses and flowers, and stepped onto the stone foundation of what must at one time have been a huge house. Apparently, Rose used to have a neighbor that lived just minutes away. I wondered what had happened to the house. Besides the foundation and the chimney, there was no sign of the rest of the structure, no fixtures, no lumber, nothing to indicate what had once stood on this site.

I looked all around me. The house would have had a view of the lake, but now bunches of saplings had grown up, blocking the line of sight to the water. I turned and looked back in the direction I'd come, and a reflection of some sort caught my eye. I picked my way carefully through the field, and re-entered the forest maybe twenty feet inland from where I'd emerged. I wove my way around the twisted roots of a fallen tree, and suddenly, a tiny, beautiful Victorian cottage came into view. It was so unexpected and so charmingly quaint that for a moment, I thought I had to be imagining it. Only once I approached it and rested my palm against the peeled paint of the door did it stop feeling like a mirage.

One look at the door handle, and I knew immediately that my key would fit. It was the same ornate brass as the key, fanciful and pretty. I hesitated for a moment. This was it, the last place where I might possibly find out anything about the man in the photograph. I didn't know which would be worse – finding out all about him from this place, or finding nothing at all. Which of these options would actually lay my obsession to rest?

The slender key slid easily into place and I took a deep breath, then turned it. The door unlocked with a sharp click. I left the key in the lock, and gave the door a little push. It swung open on rusty hinges.

My breath caught, and one word flew from my lips before I could stop it. "Nikolai."

Chapter Seven

It felt as if the whole world had shifted underneath me. I took a hesitant step into the dim interior of the Victorian cottage, my eyes gradually adjusting to the low light.

For a few precious seconds, I thought I'd seen Nikolai standing before me.

But what I'd seen was a portrait of him. It was on an easel, angled toward the weak sunlight that found its way in through the filthy windowpanes.

Rose had never finished this painting. The bottom few inches were still plain canvas. But the likeness she'd captured was so similar to the photo that her talent was unmistakable.

The smell of oil paint still hung in the room, and I touched the painting gingerly when I picked it up. But that was ridiculous, of course. It had dried decades ago. I carried it outside with me, into the light, to have a better look at it.

He appeared to be the same age in this portrait as he'd been in the photograph. In the photo he'd been posed, serious, and this was another side of him entirely. Here, Nikolai was smiling, his eyes sparkling, his hair tousled. He was heartbreakingly beautiful.

I'd wondered what color his eyes were, only being able to tell they were light in the black and white photo. Now I saw they were the palest, clearest aquamarine. Rose had painted this portrait with absolute photorealism, but she had to have taken a bit of artistic license with that color. No one had eyes like that.

I sat on the ground, leaning against the cottage, and held the painting on my lap. And I stared at it long and hard.

It was too perfect. *He* was too perfect. This type of beauty didn't exist – not now, not back then. The photo I'd found had probably somehow been retouched, some old trick of the trade to make his skin so flawless and luminous, his hair so glossy and black, his eyes so brilliant and intense. Apparently that retouched photo was what Rose had been remembering as well when she went to do his portrait. No way could this be accurate.

I'd been mourning this man that had been and gone, bemoaning, insanely, the fact that time and circumstance had kept me from him. But maybe what had drawn me with such magnetic force was something that had never existed at all, something conjured in a photography studio, and then again with a paintbrush.

Not that it was just his beauty that had drawn me in. It was something far deeper, some pull, some connection I couldn't begin to explain. But I tried to ignore that part of it now as I attempted to rationalize away my obsession.

I stood and brushed off the seat of my shorts, then leaned the painting against the wall and went around the outside of the cottage. The side of the building facing the former house was inset with several large windows, now nearly opaque behind decades of dirt and pollen and cobwebs. I looked around me and picked up a fluffy, recently fallen pine bough, and used it as a primitive feather duster on the glass. It worked fairly well, and when I went back inside the cottage, it was far lighter than it had been initially. I set the painting back on its easel, and looked around me. And realized Rose had been as obsessed as I was.

Two of the walls were covered floor to ceiling in photos, drawings and watercolors. All of one subject. All of Nikolai. I gasped, my heart leaping in my chest, my hand flying to my mouth.

This wasn't a studio. It was a shrine.

Rose had kept her obsession confined here, in this space. She'd kept it a secret from Chad, her friend and housekeeper, who hadn't been allowed in here. And she'd only brought that one photo into her home, a small concession to the madness that must have gripped her just as surely as it had me.

Was it this obsession that had kept her isolated out here for most of her life, away from the world, away from other people? Was this what had stopped her from marrying, from having a family of her own? She'd been quite obviously in love with this man, and maybe that had cost her everything.

I hesitated before stepping closer to the walls. The shrine. Oh God.

In picture after picture, he was pure, ethereal beauty. If anything, that first photo and that portrait didn't do him justice. Intelligence and humor burned in his pale blue eyes. Grace and strength were unmistakable in the powerful lines of his body. He was perfection. And he filled me with a longing so deep, so profound that I wondered how I'd ever get past it.

"Nikolai." Again the word came from me on its own. A prayer. A wish.

I sunk to my knees and carefully unpinned a drawing from the wall, studying it closely, memorizing it, before replacing it and selecting another. I did this with drawing after drawing, photo after photo, reveling in this man, aching for him with every part of me.

A pretty young woman with dark, shoulder-length hair was in a handful of the photos along with Nikolai. That had to be Rose. I already knew she was fairly petite based on the dresses hanging in her closet, but she looked downright tiny next to this man, so obviously he had been quite tall. She'd been young when these photos were taken, probably in her mid-twenties. In every picture she was smiling brightly, her dark eyes alight. She'd been so happy. But this happiness would have been short-lived, I knew. For whatever reason, Nikolai and Rose didn't get a happily ever after.

My heart broke for her. I couldn't imagine having this man and then losing him, I couldn't imagine surviving it. But she had. Rose Azzetti had obviously been a strong woman. Yes, she chose to remain isolated up here, but by all accounts, this loss hadn't destroyed her. Irv had described her as kind and loving. Chad had called her a hell of a gal. Rose somehow had gone on, despite the obvious obsession that led her to assemble this shrine.

Hours passed as I studied one photo after another, drinking in Nikolai. Eventually it became too dark to see. It was also too dark to find my way back to the lake house by then, I realized, so I curled up on a dusty old upholstered chair to spend the night there in the studio.

Sleep eluded me, and as I shivered in the dark and cold, I thought long and hard about my situation. I could go crazy with my longing for this man. I'd never, ever get enough of him. It was a disturbing realization.

I tucked my knees up under my chin and hugged my legs tightly. It was so stupid that I'd stayed here until nightfall. I'd never been particularly afraid of the dark, but out here in this little cottage, the darkness was so absolute that it was unnerving. It didn't help that I yet again had the distinct feeling of being watched, which apparently was a symptom of my particular brand of crazy.

Mercifully, I did manage to doze off at some point. And when I awoke at first light, shivering and hungry, I leapt up quickly, not allowing myself to look back at the drawings and photos, dropping the picture I realized I'd been clutching. I dashed from the cottage, pulling the door shut behind me, and plunged into the woods. The uneven terrain tripped me up a couple times, and it felt like ages before I emerged back into the clearing around Rose's modern lake house.

I climbed into bed, pulling the covers over my head. But it was no better here. The shrine called to me from across the woods, beckoning me back to lose myself in the madness, to worship at the altar of Nikolai, to give in to the aching need to experience every bit of him I possibly could.

I needed to get away from here.

I jumped out of bed, grabbed my duffle bag and backpack from the floor, and quickly packed up my few possessions. For an insane moment, I thought about bringing Nikolai's photo, the one that had started all of this. Yeah, no.

When I got downstairs, I hesitated for a moment in the middle of the living room. What was I doing? Where was I going? I'd only gotten as far as *I need to get away* in my thinking. Was I going to drive back to Long Beach and move in with my mom and brothers in Irv's condo? Was I going to give up the lake house so soon?

I really loved it here. I thought about the sheer happiness of days spent drawing in the sun with no responsibilities, no worries. What a rare, incredible gift those days had been.

As soon as I went back I'd need to find work again, some variation on the countless dull, meaningless jobs I'd had since I was fourteen. And I'd need to re-enroll in college, try to salvage something of those wasted four years. I had such incredible freedom now, and it was going to end all too soon anyway. Cutting my time here short would be a huge loss.

Plus, if I was running because I feared for my sanity, well, hurrying back to southern California to live with my family wasn't exactly the road to mental health.

It occurred to me then that maybe I didn't have to go for good. I probably just needed a change of scenery for a couple days. Maybe that would do the trick, give me the opportunity to clear my head and gain a little perspective. It was worth a shot.

Chapter Eight

It took over an hour to wind my way down the dirt road and then drive out of the mountains and to the coast. I emerged onto Highway One and drove south for a while, finally parking at a deserted beach. The steady rhythm of the waves against the shore was really soothing, and I ended up spending all day alternately walking and running in the sand for miles and miles.

That night, I checked into a little motel across the highway from the beach. The place was definitely on the old and run-down side, but it worked with my meager budget. My room had a tiny patio out back with a plastic table and chair, and I made myself comfortable out there. A strong breeze was coming off the ocean, and I closed my eyes and let myself relax as I breathed in the sea air. I realized after a while that I'd apparently gotten over the constant nagging sensation of being watched. I'd been beginning to wonder if that particular insanity was a permanent part of me now.

When it got too cold to stay outside, I zoned out in front of the television, something I hadn't been able to do at the lake. Finally I fell asleep fully clothed to the sound of some inane sitcom.

And I awoke at dawn. Really? This room was perfectly dark, I could have slept in. Except apparently, I was now running on lake house time.

A second night in the motel would have used up too much of my money, so I took a long run along the shore, then showered and changed and checked out of my room. Breakfast came from Seven-Eleven, and then I drove north to a pretty beach and spent the day alternately sunbathing and bodysurfing in the bracingly cold Pacific.

It was late afternoon by the time I left the beach. I was wet and sandy, and really didn't want to drive back to the lake house like this. So I stopped at a gas station and grabbed a change of clothes from my duffle bag, then headed to the men's room at the back of the building.

There were two stalls, neither of which had doors. One was occupied. I turned my back to the stalls and pulled my soggy t-shirt over my head, rinsing it in the sink and ringing it out, then tried to scrub the sand off my hands and arms. It clung tenaciously.

"Looks like you brought half the beach in here with you," a voice behind me said. His tone was light, friendly.

I barely glanced at the other man in the restroom and said, "Yeah, it feels that way."

"You live in town?"

"No, just visiting," I told him, still concentrating on the sand.

I jumped at the touch of the man's hand on my back and met his eyes in the gouged, distorted glass of the bathroom mirror. He was taller and heavier than I was, maybe in his mid-thirties and not bad-looking, if somewhat nondescript. He seemed nonthreatening, despite the fact that his hand was on my body. "You're cute," he said with a friendly smile. "It's a shame you don't live in town."

Oh my God, he's hitting on me, I thought with utter shock. Nobody had hit on me since Donnie.

I turned around and again met this stranger's gaze. He said in a low voice, still smiling amicably, "Why don't you be a good boy and take care of this for me?"

For a moment, I stupidly didn't know what he meant. And then my gaze slid down his body to his other hand. He was stroking his cock, which jutted out of his unzipped fly.

A mixture of emotions ricocheted through me, fear and panic only slightly drowned out by something else: the throb of my own cock in response to what I was watching. I stood rooted in place, half of me wanting to bolt for the door, the other half wanting to drop to my knees as I watched him work his hard shaft.

Finally, he made the decision for me. He pushed me down with a firm hand on my shoulder and I knelt before him. I hesitated, looking up at him, and he thrust his cock into my face. Automatically, my lips parted.

Sucking his cock was alien and familiar at the same time. This was how Donnie used to take me too, just pushing me onto my knees with no preamble. My own cock throbbed in my wet swim trunks, but I ignored it. Even as part of my brain screamed at me to stop, I continued the blow job, remembering all that my ex had taught me over the years. The taste was different than Donnie, but not unpleasant. This man's cock was a little smaller too, and I found I could deep-throat him easily.

He was getting close to cumming, and I started to pull off so I could finish him with my hand, since I had no intention of swallowing his load. But this man had other ideas. All of a sudden he pushed me back, pinning my head against the wall. He grabbed two big handfuls of my hair and started to fuck my mouth, hard, as he moaned with pleasure. I struggled, choking, panicking, but it was too late – already the first shot of cum was hitting the back of my throat. He kept pounding into me as I tried to cry out, tried to pull away. It was no use.

The stranger didn't let go of me until he was completely spent. When he finally pulled out of my mouth, I fell to my hands and knees, coughing, gasping for air, tears streaming down my face. He zipped his pants and left without a word.

I struggled to my feet and rinsed my mouth out at the sink, bringing water to my bruised lips with a shaking hand. My clothes, the clean ones and the wet shirt, were all in a pile on the dirty floor. Somehow I had the presence of mind to grab them, then hesitated for a moment with my hand on the door handle. Would that man be out there waiting for me? Even worse, would he come back in here and do something else to me?

That thought sent me running to my car, and I sped in the direction of the lake house. My body was shaking, my mind a blur. Belatedly, fear crashed into me and my flight response kicked in, and I pressed the accelerator.

I tried to calm down and figure out what had just happened as I drove. It hadn't been rape. I'd said yes…well, I hadn't said no, anyway. At first…at first it had been pleasurable, and I'd liked the fact that someone wanted me. It had just become frightening toward the end, when he got rough and when I felt I had absolutely no control.

I was scared and shaken, but I was also furious with myself, especially because my own body had betrayed me. Instead of thinking clearly and getting myself out of a potentially dangerous situation, I'd gotten aroused. And then I let myself get used, treated like a whore, and tossed aside. What the fuck was wrong with me?

It seemed to take days to get back to the lake house. I held it together until I pulled up behind the house and unlocked the door with a shaking hand. It was such a relief to be back here. Why had I ever left? I locked the door behind me, and dropped the keys onto a side table.

Home. I was home. I was safe.

I ran upstairs and turned the shower hotter than I could stand it and stood under it, scrubbing my skin until the water ran cold. I was still wearing my swim trunks and sneakers, and when I realized this I kicked them off and pushed them into a corner of the shower, and then I scrubbed myself some more. I stepped out long enough to grab a toothbrush and toothpaste, then got back under the water and scrubbed my teeth so hard that the brush snapped in half.

The water had long since become freezing cold, and I was shaking violently when I finally got out of the shower. I didn't even bother to towel off. I just headed for the kitchen, leaving a trail of water behind me.

I needed oblivion. The most direct route was the Jack Daniels in the cabinet, and I stood dripping on the kitchen floor as I tossed the lid aside and drank right from the bottle. I rested my hand on the kitchen counter, and pulled back suddenly as I felt something under my palm. It was the studio key. I didn't remember putting it there...something seemed off about that. But then I'd been in such a state when leaving Nikolai's shrine that I really couldn't remember what exactly I'd done afterwards. I took another long drink from the bottle, the whiskey burning all the way down. I coughed a bit, but then returned the bottle to my lips.

I was pretty sure I'd fallen asleep on the cold, hard kitchen floor, but now I was in my bed. It was pitch dark and the booze was still coursing through my system, making everything fuzzy. And there were big, strong arms around me. Ah, I knew this dream. "Nikolai," I whispered.

"Nathaniel." His voice was so soft, so beautiful. He had a very faint accent, of an origin I couldn't quite pinpoint.

"This is my favorite dream," I told him, still quite drunk.

"Is it?" He stroked my hair gently and I nodded and nestled against his shoulder. I was on his lap as he sat propped up in bed, held like one holds a child, the warm red blanket wrapped securely around both of us.

"Sometimes I think I never want to wake up," I murmured. "I just want to stay asleep forever so you'll keep holding me."

"Don't say that, darling. You know you need to wake up."

"Not yet," I gasped, and his arms tightened around me.

"No. Not yet." He went back to stroking my hair. After a while he whispered, "What happened, Nathaniel? What happened after you left here?"

"I don't know." I buried my face in his shoulder, full of shame, and grabbed handfuls of his soft shirt.

"Did someone hurt you?"

"Yes. I let him."

"You let someone hurt you?"

"I didn't know he was going to hurt me." I thought about it for a minute. "I guess…I guess he didn't really hurt me. I just got scared when he got rough with me."

"What did he do to you?"

A little whimper escaped me. "Don't make me tell you, Nikolai. Please. I'm so ashamed."

"Shhhh, baby, it's okay." He started rocking me, holding me securely.

I whispered, "I don't know why I let people treat me like that, first Donnie, then that stranger. They were the only two men that ever even gave me a second look, the only two that ever even *saw* me. And all they wanted was to use me to get off. Maybe that's all I'm good for."

"Don't say that, Nathaniel."

"Why not? It's true. No one's ever going to want me for more than that, no one's ever gonna think I'm worth more."

"I *know* you're worth more, baby."

"You're just a beautiful dream, Nikolai. And it's so incredibly pointless to wish you were real, because even if you were, it's not like you'd want anything to do with me. Even if we had existed in the same place and time, you would have been completely out of my league, you'd never have given me the time of day."

"That's absolutely untrue."

I chuckled a little at that. "I don't know where this dream is even coming from. I have absolutely no self-esteem. So why on earth is my subconscious trying to make me feel better?"

Nikolai sighed and tightened his arms around me.

"I feel so safe here," I murmured after a while.

He said quietly, "You're not."

I raised my head and tried to look him in the eye, but it was too dark to see his face. "I'm not?"

"No, baby. You should leave here. Go back home. Tomorrow, when you've sobered up and can drive safely."

"Will you come with me?" My voice sounded so small to me.

"I wish I could."

"I don't really have a home to go back to," I admitted. "Even if I did, I'd still want to stay here."

"Why?"

"Because this is where your memory lives. This is where I can be close to you."

A pause. Then, "You don't even know me, Nathaniel."

"No. But God, I wish I did."

"Am I all that's keeping you here?"

"No. I love it here. I love the house and the deck and the lake. I want to stay."

He paused to consider this, then asked, "How long?"

"Until the end of summer. Then I'll have to go back and face reality." I snuggled against his shoulder.

"Okay," he said after a moment. "I can stay away until then."

"No!" I tried to sit up, but he swung us around effortlessly so I was lying beside him, my body pressed against the length of his, his arms holding me gently but firmly.

"Shhhh," his voice washed over me. "Settle down, baby."

"I don't want you to stay away."

"I know. Just relax, sweetheart."

And I did, just from his words, as if they somehow had power over me. "Don't stay away." I rubbed my cheek against him and murmured as my thoughts grew ever hazier, "Besides, you're not even really here. You died a long time ago, I'm just dreaming you. How would you stay away?"

He stroked my hair and whispered, "Go to sleep, Nathaniel."

"I *am* asleep."

*****

The next morning, I awoke hung over and disoriented. God, what a weird, vivid dream. And absolutely wonderful. I wrapped myself tightly in the blanket, trying to recreate the feeling of Nikolai's arms around me.

And I thought back over our 'conversation.' Dreams were supposed to have meaning. So what the hell did any of that mean? *I'm not safe here*…. Okay, I was obsessing over a dead man, and at night I dreamt I was talking to his ghost. Clearly I was losing my mind, so my declining mental health had to be the threat to my safety.

Beyond that…yeah, no clue.

Chapter Nine

It was the second week of June and I'd been at the lake for about two months. Bill and Chad were at the house, having once again brought me a ton of groceries – way too much this time, more than usual. When I questioned them on it, Chad just grinned and said, "You might need it."

They also brought word from my family. I hadn't gone anywhere since that one fateful trip to the coast, which meant I hadn't had cell phone reception. But the housekeeper and his great grandson had become my own personal pony express, carrying messages back and forth between my family and me. I learned that Irv was taking my mom and brothers on some sort of family getaway now that my brothers were out of school, and that all were well.

What also made this a banner day were the new art supplies that Bill and Chad had decided to get for me. I carried my treasure around to the little table on the deck while the two of them attempted to cram a year's worth of food into the refrigerator. The supplies included an amazing set of colored pencils in a wooden carrying case, which were actually too beautiful to use. I'd probably freaked Bill out when I grabbed him in a big hug of gratitude after he gave me the pencils. He must have thought all my time alone was sending me off the deep end.

But instead of going stone-cold crazy out in the woods, I was actually doing pretty well. I'd been coping with the isolation by spending most of my time drawing, sometimes for hours at a time, lost in the world brought to life on my sketch pad. It was gratifying to watch my skills dramatically improving with practice.

And the thing that *could* have been driving me insane, well, that I tackled one day at a time.

In order for me to stay here at the lake house through the end of summer, I knew I had to get over my obsession with Nikolai. Step one in that particular recovery program had been to stay the hell away from Rose's art studio. I hadn't gone back since the day I discovered it and spent hours obsessing over picture after picture. It'd be like a recovering alcoholic hanging out in a bar: I knew it was way too much for me to handle.

Though that first photograph still lived in my nightstand, I more or less stayed away from it, too. Only sometimes, late at night when the quiet solitude got to be too much, would I allow myself a look at the photo. The longing it stirred up was intense, but somehow that was better than just feeling empty.

Aside from that, there were signs that my mental health recovery program was working. For one thing, I no longer had that nagging feeling of being watched all the time, which must have been the first stage of some sort of mental breakdown. And okay, I still had intense sex dreams about Nikolai, but I no longer dreamt he was holding me, talking to me. Maybe that was progress, somehow.

A far-off engine caught my attention and I looked up from my art supplies, wondering if Chad and Bill had driven off when I hadn't been paying attention. But no, their white SUV was still parked under the big redwood tree.

The sound was gradually increasing – very gradually, as whoever was coming tried to negotiate the rutted dirt road. It was a few minutes before a big blue Ford Bronco appeared around the last bend and pulled up beside Bill's vehicle.

And then my family was spilling out of the car, bickering and complaining. Irv saw me and waved, smiling happily, then went around and opened my mother's door for her while my three little brothers piled out of the back seat.

Besides Irv, the only other family member that was smiling was my youngest brother, Ryan. He yelled, "Thaniel!" when he saw me, and ran into my arms.

"Hey buddy!" I exclaimed, grabbing him up in a big hug and swinging him around.

"Surprise!" he yelled. "Are you surprised?"

I set him on the ground and knelt in front of him, holding him by the shoulders, and said, "Yes! Wow, look at you! Did you grow a foot since last time I saw you?"

He scowled. "No. I was the shortest one in kindergarten. 'Cept for the girls. I'm on summer vacation now." Six year old Ryan was a grubby little angel with dark brown hair and eyes. I absolutely adored him. He said sternly, "Are you wearing your friendship bracelets? Let me see." I held out both my wrists to him, and his face erupted into a huge smile. "You *are* wearing them!"

"Of course I am! I never take them off. You know that." The faded and worn out bits of string were my most prized possessions.

"I made you a new one!" He dug in the pocket of his shorts, then triumphantly held up a woven strip of blue and yellow threads. But his little face clouded over. "Tyler and Travis said they're for girls." Those were my two middle brothers. We called them the twins, even though they were born thirteen months apart. They had the same dad, and their father, unlike the rest of ours, made an occasional appearance in their lives. Which was too bad, because he was a grade-A douche bag. I hoped his douchey tendencies weren't rubbing off on his sons.

"Tyler and Travis are wrong." I held my right wrist out for him. "Here, put it on this hand. Then I'll have three bracelets on each side." He smiled again, then concentrated on the task of tying nice, tight knots to secure the bracelet permanently to my wrist.

"Thank you," I said sincerely when he'd finished. I held my arm up and examined the uneven little diamond pattern. "This is by far the coolest bracelet ever. And no way is it for girls."

He threw his arms around my neck and said, "I missed you, Thaniel."

"Me too, buddy. I missed you so much." I gave him a big hug, then stood up and grabbed his hand. "Come on, I want to say hi to everybody."

"Patrick didn't come," he told me as we walked hand in hand toward the Bronco, where Irv was extracting a mountain of luggage. "Cuz he has a *girlfriend*." Ryan scrunched up his face in disgust. Girls were still gross at age six.

"He does?" I was surprised at that. Apparently I still thought of my brother Patrick as a kid. But he was actually seventeen, he'd be a high school senior next year.

"Her name's Cora, and all they ever do is mwah! Mwah! Mwah!" Ryan made an exaggerated kissy face, eyes squinched shut, lips jutting out.

I laughed and said, "Gross!"

"Yeah! It's totally gross!"

By now we'd reached the rented Bronco, and I shook Irv's hand. "Hey. Nice surprise."

He slung the strap of a tote bag over his shoulder and smiled warmly at me. "Hiya Nate. Hope this is okay. You've been pretty isolated up here and we thought you could use a little family time, so we decided to surprise you."

"It's wonderful to see all of you," I said, grabbing two suitcases.

"Patrick didn't come."

"Yeah, Ryan told me."

Irv shrugged. "Young love, whatcha gonna do?"

We carried the bags inside, where my mother was trying to placate Tyler and Travis. They'd immediately noticed the lack of a television, and were pitching a fit. They were eleven and twelve, and I was pretty sure no TV constituted cruel and unusual punishment at that age. When my mom caught sight of me, she tried to distract the twins by saying, "Shut up a minute and say hi to your brother."

"Hey Nate," Travis said. "How the hell haven't you killed yourself after living without TV for two months?" He was kind of a smartass.

I thought our mom was going to yell at him for swearing, but she just sighed and said, "Boys, why don't you go explore? Just don't wander off into the woods, okay? There might be bears."

Tyler sighed and said, "Yeah, right." But they did as they were told and slouched out of the house.

Ryan, who was still holding my hand, stared after his brothers and told me, "They started their own club. It's called T-n-T. They won't let me join."

Typical. I told him, "Well, you know what? We can start our own club, and *they* can't join." That earned me another radiant smile.

"Hey Ry, you want juice?" Irv called from the kitchen, shaking a little green box, and Ryan launched himself after it.

My mom was looking at me closely, and in lieu of saying hello she said, "You're going to get skin cancer."

"What?"

"Look how tan you are. I bet you haven't been using sunscreen."

"Mom, it's fine," I said, rolling my eyes. "I don't think I'm going to keel over tomorrow from melanoma." I immediately felt like I was ten years old.

She was still studying me closely. "You look good though. You're not as skinny as before, your muscles have filled out a bit. Have you been running?"

"Every day."

"I haven't seen your hair that blonde since you were Ryan's age. It suits you." She held my gaze and asked, "Have you been okay all alone up here?"

"Yeah. Great, actually."

She watched me for another few moments and seemed to decide I was telling the truth, because she nodded and said, "Well, good. I wasn't sure about this idea of Irv's, sending you off to the middle of nowhere. I don't think he was too sure, either. That's why he wanted to come check on you."

"It's been great here, Mom. Really."

"Have you gotten over Donnie?"

"Yeah. It still hurts a little when I think about him. Maybe it always will. But I know now that relationship was never going to go anywhere. He was never going to care about me the same way I cared about him. So I'm actually kind of glad it ended." I studied the floor as I said that, and my mom reached out and gave my shoulder a squeeze.

"Stella, I just opened a bottle of Zinfandel," Irv called from the kitchen. "Want me to pour you a glass?"

"God Irving, after that miserable dirt road, just hand me the whole bottle," my mom said. And then she grinned at him in a way that made me really happy. All was obviously well between the two of them.

I followed her to the kitchen and perched on a barstool as wine was handed around, and accepted a glass from Irv. I generally thought wine was disgusting, but I thought I'd give it another chance. I took a cautious sip and grimaced. Ugh, yeah, still disgusting.

Bill and Chad were settled comfortably beside me at the breakfast bar, and Irv handed both of them glasses of wine. Obviously they'd been in on this little surprise, and it explained the insane amount of food they'd brought.

Chad and Irv were catching up on old times, and I saw now that Irv was far more than an employer. He was practically family. Apparently Irv had spent almost every summer here as a kid, visiting his aunt. So since Chad had been employed by Aunt Rose for decades, Irv had known him most of his life. "I used to love coming here as a kid," Irv told me. "Well, you know, back then it was at the old house, but still, here at the lake. It felt like a different planet from Hoboken."

"At the old house?" I echoed.

"Yeah. Aunt Rose used to have a big Victorian that she inherited from her father. It burned down in the early 1960's, and then she built this place."

"Oh. Was it just south of here?" That must have been the foundation beside the art studio, not a neighbor's house after all.

"Yeah. It was a great old house, but dark, too dark for Rose's taste. When she built this place, all she wanted was sunshine."

Beginning at the crack of dawn every day, I thought ruefully.

Chad and Bill stayed for dinner. Irv cooked up mountains of Shrimp Scampi, and we carried chairs out to the deck and ate on our laps as a wonderful breeze blew in off the lake. After dinner, the boys ran around whooping and hollering in the field. I was glad to see the two older boys were including Ryan. The 'grownups' meanwhile started talking about California politics, which was so boring that I decided to join the other group, and spent the rest of the evening running around playing freeze tag with my brothers.

My family stayed for five days. I slept on the couch with my brothers lined up in sleeping bags beside me on the living room floor, Irv and my mom upstairs in 'my' bed. Since the whole house was wide open, stairs leading directly into the bedroom with no door between us, I awoke every morning to the sound of my mom grumbling, "Oh Christ, if I never see another sunrise it'll be too soon."

And then before I knew it, the visit was over and they were packing up the car. Ryan stood teary eyed, clinging to the hem of my shirt, and I knelt down and hugged him for a long time. Then I handed him the cardboard box I'd been holding. "Here, buddy. I made you a present."

To the top of the green cardboard box that used to contain the typing paper, I'd glued a drawing of a coat-of-arms. It was the logo for the Ryan Club, which we'd founded over the last few days. He was wide-eyed when he lifted the lid, and then his entire face was taken up with his radiant smile.

I'd given Ryan five comic books that I'd drawn for him over the past several weeks – all pictures, since he didn't really read yet. And on top of the comic books were four official-looking ID cards that I'd laminated with clear packing tape. "Whoa!" he exclaimed. "What are these?"

"Identification cards, only for members of the Ryan Club." I held a card up and pointed at it. "See, this one has your picture, and here it says your name, and that you're president of the club. On that one's my name, and it says I'm vice president. So our club is official now. The other two cards are for Travis and Tyler. I'll bet they'd like to join the club, too. But they can only join if they're nice to you."

"Awesome!" He handed me the card with the cartoon of me on it and said gravely, "You better keep this someplace safe." I took the card from him and assured him I would as I slid it into the pocket of my t-shirt.

By now the rest of the family had lined up at the car. "Quick, secret handshake!" I told Ryan, and we went through the elaborate series of gestures that we'd spent five days perfecting.

"I'm gonna miss you, Thaniel."

"I'm gonna miss you too, buddy. But I'll see you in a couple months, at the end of summer," I promised, and he nodded.

After that I went down the line and hugged each of my family members. I hesitated when I got to Irv, but he grabbed me in a hug and slapped my back. "Kid," he said, "I'm proud of you. I think you're doing great up here. And this drawing thing, you really got something there." I had been too embarrassed to show him any of my artwork. But I'd shown Ryan, who promptly went running with one of my sketchbooks to my mom and Irv, beaming with delight as he exclaimed, "Look what my big brother can do!"

Soon everyone was in the car, waving goodbye as the rented Ford swung around in a wide arc. As they headed for the dirt road I heard my mother exclaim through her open window, "Christ, here we go again," and then shriek as the big SUV hit the first deep rut.

And Irv chuckled and replied, "I know, sweetheart. I'll make it up to ya."

It took a while for them to make it far enough down the road so that I no longer heard the SUV's engine. And then, silence descended like it had been hiding around the corner, waiting until my family left.

Okay, it wasn't really silent, I mused, as I walked around to the deck and gathered up a couple cups and juice boxes. There was the constant hum of frogs and crickets, the gentle rustle of a breeze through the grasses in the field, even the occasional splash of a fish in the lake jumping for an insect. But it was incredibly peaceful, and I realized I'd missed this quiet chorus.

I went into the kitchen, and grinned at the sight of the refrigerator. It was totally covered in drawings, mostly done by Ryan. But a few were by Travis and Tyler as well, who'd at first scoffed at Ryan's and my daily art projects, and later asked to join in. My favorite was one of Ryan and me holding hands. My second favorite was of our family of seven (including Irv), where Ryan had drawn every single one of us dressed as Iron Man.

I noticed then that something else had been tacked to the fridge when I wasn't looking. Someone had helped my little brother write *I love you Nate, from Ryan* in shaky six year old handwriting. Every letter was a different color – he'd thoroughly enjoyed my beautiful new set of colored pencils, which I'd gladly let him use even though I wouldn't have let myself use them.

I sat on the floor and leaned against the kitchen island, hugging my knees to my chest, looking at the drawings, the note, all that love. So often, I felt alone. Adrift. But I really wasn't. I had a family that loved and accepted me. I was incredibly lucky.

Things hadn't been that great growing up. Like I said before, my dad took off when I was three, I couldn't even remember him. And then all these other men filtered through our lives as my mom remarried again and again. Just about the time I'd start to get attached to one of these new dads, he'd take off, too. That wasn't so easy when I was a kid.

Sure, my mom was there throughout. But she was always so wrapped up in her own drama, cheerful and loving when things were going well, withdrawn when her relationships started to go awry. Things were great now, she was happy because she had Irv. That's just how she was, changing with the tides.

God, I hoped this one worked out for her. Irv was such a good guy, and I wanted their relationship to last not only for Stella's sake, but for the boys as well. The kids needed a dad. It would be so nice if my brothers could grow up feeling a sense of stability and security. They deserved that.

I looked at Ryan's drawings again. He was an amazing kid, and I missed him already. I really didn't understand the hero worship thing that he had going on, why he thought I was so special. He made me want to be a better person, someone deserving of the pedestal he put me on. Maybe someday, I'd be worthy of it. But I still had a long way to go.

Chapter Ten

It had been a week since my family left and I was in a funk.

I couldn't quite settle back into the regular pattern I'd been in before. The worst part was that I couldn't draw either, and that had been how I'd spent most of my time prior to their visit. Apparently I was experiencing the artist's equivalent of writer's block, and would just sit there staring at my blank sketchpads. I just couldn't concentrate, and the same went for reading.

About the only thing I could do was exercise, and I pushed myself to run faster and farther than ever before. I started swimming, too, out in the lake. It was bitterly cold, and each time I jumped in, the water was like an electric shock to my system. Though once I got warmed up, it actually felt pretty good.

But my body could only take so much abuse. I couldn't spend all day every day running and swimming. And for the last two days it had been raining heavily, so I could do absolutely nothing at all.

I was incredibly restless, and thought maybe I should get in the car and go somewhere, try a change of scenery. But then I decided against it. It wasn't fear over what had happened last time that kept me here. It was the knowledge that I really didn't know where to go or what I'd do once I got there.

When I tried to go to bed and put the day out of its misery, I just lay wide awake, listening to the tapping of the rain on the roof. Throughout my life, off and on, I'd struggled with insomnia, and in the last few days, it had returned with a vengeance. This was especially rough since I had to wake up at sunrise, and on nights where I couldn't fall asleep until three or four in the morning, dawn came *way* too early. I was so desperate to get some sleep that I had even tried sleeping blindfolded with one of Aunt Rose's scarves to keep the light out, but it didn't help at all. Nothing did.

It was well after midnight on this particular night. I'd been pacing the house like an oh-so-clichéd caged animal, and when I'd tired of pacing, I'd somehow ended up stretching out on my back on Rose's big dining table, staring up at the high ceiling.

I needed…something. I didn't know what. I reached down and experimentally rubbed my cock through my thin flannel pajama bottoms, and while it responded with a kind of half-hearted throb, I just couldn't muster the enthusiasm somehow. A line from a Green Day song came to mind: "When masturbation's lost its fun, you're fucking lonely."

"Well *that* song sums up my life right now," I murmured, and then sighed and rolled my eyes. I was both talking to myself and quoting song lyrics. Surely my time would be better spent getting incredibly drunk, hopefully to the point that I'd either pass out, fall asleep, or some combination thereof.

I swung myself off the table and went into the kitchen, pausing long enough to fire up Green Day on the MP3 player so I could hear tonight's theme song. Then I found a bottle of Jack Daniels and told it, "You're always such a bad idea," before throwing the lid over my shoulder and taking a swig.

After drinking a hell of a lot over the next hour, I was still annoyingly awake. And also drunk off my ass. Instead of knocking me out, the alcohol had somehow just made me more restless. I was aching with a need I knew all too well, and all my normal restraints had washed away with the alcohol.

I needed to go see Nikolai.

Here's the thing about me and drinking: at a certain blood alcohol level, I began to think that all of my ideas were brilliant. This was the level of drunkenness that in the past led me to believe

I was writing profound song lyrics, and in the morning I'd find I'd written an illiterate limerick about my testicles.

Oh yeah, I was right there.

I convinced myself that I was being rational by putting on my Converse and locating a flashlight. I even remembered the key to the art studio, and slung the ribbon it was on around my neck. *See?* My drunk-ass brain slurred. *You're totally in control because you stopped to think of those things.*

And then I was out the door.

It was drizzling, but I didn't care. I needed to do this. I just needed a few minutes in the studio with Nikolai's pictures. That was all. I wanted him. I needed him. And thanks to my good friend Jack Daniels, I could think of absolutely no reason not to indulge, to give myself what I needed.

I tried to keep the flashlight's beam steady as I rounded the corner of the house and half-jogged past the garage and into the woods. I knew which way to go. All I had to do was keep the lake to my right.

Okay, I couldn't actually *see* the lake right now in the dark, but that was fine. This was the right way. And if I missed the studio, I'd still come out into that big clearing where the old house had stood, and then I could find the studio from there.

Piece of cake.

Easy peasy.

No problemo.

How long had I been walking?

The woods were really annoying. Tree roots seemed to exist only to trip me. Plants scratched my arms and bare torso. "I fucking hate nature," I mumbled, and barely avoided colliding with a tree branch, which I then told to fuck off (I also became quite foul-mouthed when I was drunk).

It was right around here somewhere. I'd find the studio any minute. And I wasn't going to stay long. I decided I was going to gather up a big armload of Nikolai's photos and drawings and bring them back to the house, where I could lay them all over the bed and curl up with them.

Why had I been denying myself this? What was the harm? This idea was *fine*. What could go wrong?

Only, the studio wasn't where it should be. Or maybe *I* wasn't where I should be. Shouldn't I have come to the clearing by now?

Maybe I just needed to walk a little farther.

And a little farther.

The flashlight tried to fade out, but I shook it and it brightened up again. I had to be close. Right? Any moment now I'd come out into the clearing.

It took an inordinately long time for the first skitter of panic to find its way down my spine.

I was lost.

Fear spiked in me, and my flight response kicked in. I whirled around and began running back through the woods. Some insane still-drunk part of me reasoned that running was good, I'd get out of the woods faster. I tripped and landed on my knees, hard. The flashlight flicked and went off when it hit the ground, and I shook it violently. It came back as a faint yellow glow. But that was something, at least.

Panic gripped me like a hand around my throat, and I leapt up and went faster still, as fast as I could in the heavy undergrowth. Then I stopped abruptly. I pushed my wet hair out of my eyes and looked around. The rain fell quietly, straight down, no wind to carry it. My breathing sounded incredibly loud to me.

Okay, think. *Focus*. It wasn't pitch dark. There was a little bit of moonlight filtering through the clouds. Not a lot, but enough to make out the shapes of trees and bushes around me. God, where was I? The forest all looked the same. There were no landmarks.

But over there…over to my left past the surrounding vegetation there was just darkness – no trees, nothing. It had to be the lake. And if I got to it, I could follow the shore back to the house. I took off running.

Just as I reached the void, my toe caught on something and I started to fall. But I didn't hit the ground – not right away. I hurtled through nothingness, airborne for just a moment.

In the next instant my body slammed violently into rocks, into hard-packed earth, the air forced from my lungs. I was rolling end over end downhill, and as soon as I could drag a breath into my body I cried out, a tiny, feeble sound.

At the bottom of the hill, my head slammed hard into the trunk of a tree, and my body came to rest tangled among its roots. I tasted blood, and I tasted the rain.

And then the darkness became absolute.

Chapter Eleven

Arms around me. Carrying me. I didn't have the energy to open my eyes. I didn't need to. I knew this dream.

"Nikolai." It was barely a whisper.

"Thank God you're awake."

"No. Not awake. Dreaming of you." My voice was almost inaudible.

"You have less survival instinct than anyone on earth. Do you know this about yourself?" He sounded angry. That made his slight accent just a little more pronounced.

"You're mad," I observed tiredly. My head was pounding, pain radiating through my body. I noted these things disinterestedly.

"Of course I'm mad! Where were you going?"

"To see you."

"What?"

"Was going to the art studio. Wanted your pictures." Talking was absolutely exhausting.

He swore vividly, in a language I didn't recognize. Then he said, "God, Nathaniel. I thought you'd gotten over that obsession."

"No. I'll never be over you." I wanted to see him, and forced my eyes open. He was totally in shadow, and moving quickly. The forest blurred around him in the weak moonlight, so fast it made me nauseous. I pressed my eyes shut again. "How can I be asleep and so tired at the same time?" I murmured.

"You're not asleep and you should try to stay awake."

"This is such a confusing dream," I muttered. "I don't understand this conversation. I don't understand what you're telling me to do."

"It's my fault. I manipulated you too many times. You can't distinguish fantasy from reality anymore."

"That's just more confusing."

I felt my body going limp then, my head rolling back on my neck. He gave me a little shake and pain shot through my body. I heard an odd, small sound, and after a moment I realized I'd whimpered.

"Nathaniel! Baby, stay with me."

A prickling sensation radiated up from my fingertips as a dull emptiness expanded to fill my chest cavity. "Nikolai...am I dying?" The words sounded like they'd come from somewhere apart from myself.

"No." His voice was hard, insistent. "You *are not* going to die. I won't let you."

It was light then on the other side of my eyelids. I felt myself being set down on a hard, cold surface. He let go of me and I wanted to reach for him, pull him back to me. But my body didn't listen to what I was telling it to do.

Water was running. Not the rain though...it wasn't falling on me anymore. Pressure on my head...something wrapped around it. My shoes and my pajama pants were being pulled off. I didn't care. Not about that, not about anything. Drifting....

Suddenly I was surrounded with warmth. Some part of my brain was still trying to piece together the sensations my body was receiving. But most of me was letting go....

"Nathaniel!" His voice was right beside me.

"Don't leave me," I murmured. "Promise you won't leave."

Strong arms tightened around me. "I promise. I'm not going anywhere, baby. And neither are you. Tilt your head back for me."

I let my head fall back from his chest. Drifting....

A warmth spread through me, radiating from the inside out. I swallowed reflexively. Some sort of liquid was in my mouth, something rich, delicious. Absolutely wonderful. I swallowed again, then mumbled, "So good. What is it?"

Softly, he said, "It's...me."

I didn't understand his answer.

Something was pressed gently against my lips. I stuck my tongue out, tasting more of whatever that was. Lapping at it. So, so good. Almost sweet to the taste. And nurturing, somehow. Healing.

My eyelids fluttered, and abruptly whatever had been pressing against my mouth was gone. I felt strong arms shift around me, holding me firmly. It was as if I was coming back to myself somehow, no longer drifting. Solid. Anchored.

I lifted my lids and stared into the most beautiful pale aquamarine eyes I'd ever seen, then jerked back so quickly that water sloshed all across the floor. I was in the lake house, in the big tub in the bathroom.

And so was Nikolai.

Chapter Twelve

Nikolai!

"What the *fuck!* What's happening? How the hell can you possibly be here?" I sputtered as I pulled away from him and retreated to one end of the tub, shaking violently, trying to figure out how to fight my way out of the insanity that had obviously completely taken over.

He stepped out of the tub and knelt beside it. He was dressed in a black t-shirt and jeans, both soaked through and clinging to his big, powerful body. Slowly he raised his hand, eyes locked on mine, acting the way one did with a frightened animal. "Shhh Nathaniel, it's okay," he said quietly as he carefully placed his hand on top of mine, which was latched onto the edge of the tub in a white-knuckled death grip. I pulled away from his touch.

"It's not okay. None of this is okay. I've either totally lost my mind, or there's a stranger in my house that looks exactly like someone who died decades ago. Both of those things are most definitely *not okay*."

His blue eyes hadn't left mine and his voice was low and soothing as he said, "Nathaniel, please. I know this is disturbing, but you almost died about two minutes ago and you're still not well. Please try to calm down."

"Tell me who you are," I demanded, trying to sound firm though my voice was shaking.

He sat back on his heels. "You already know."

"No. I don't fucking know."

He sighed and pushed his wet hair out of his eyes, leaving a streak of red across his forehead. When I saw that, I hesitated and asked, "Are...are you injured?" My sudden concern for the intruder in my bathroom was annoying, and I frowned at myself for having asked that question.

"What?" He looked at his palm, then said, "No, that's your blood. I did a terrible job trying to bandage your head wound. Will you let me try again, before you completely freak out on me?" I raised a shaking hand to my forehead and felt a wet cloth.

A long moment passed as I stared at him. He was perfectly motionless, holding my gaze, waiting. I was still hopelessly confused, but my fear was slowly draining away. Whoever this person was – this person who just happened to look like a man in an old photograph – he was obviously trying to help me, not hurt me.

I shivered and looked down at myself. Blood and dirt darkened the water in the bathtub, and a few leaves were floating on the surface. "Why am I in the tub?"

"I thought it was the quickest way to head off hypothermia."

I kept staring at the water as I tried to sort out the events of this evening. I remembered getting lost in the woods...getting hurt...there were gaps in my memory, though, and I asked quietly, "What happened tonight?"

"You ran off into the forest like a drunken lunatic and fell into a ravine."

"And...what? I died, so now I can talk to ghosts? Like Bruce Willis in that movie with the dead kid?"

He grinned a little at that, just the slightest curve at the corner of his full lips. "No. You didn't die, despite your best efforts." He stood up, turned to the cabinet behind him and pulled out a towel. "That water must be getting cold by now. Let me help you out of there before you get chilled again." He started to reach for me, but I pulled away.

"Uh, thanks Casper, but I got it." I started to stand up but my left leg collapsed under me, pain shooting through my body as I cried out. Before I could fall back into the water he scooped me into his arms effortlessly, as if I weighed nothing.

He wrapped the towel around me, then sat me gingerly on the big marble vanity. "Are you going to fall off the counter if I let go of you?" he asked, holding my gaze as his big hand pressed down on my right thigh, presumably to keep me from tipping over.

"Probably not."

He let go and watched me for a beat, then turned his back to me and peeled off his wet clothes. As he grabbed a towel for himself out of the cupboard, my gaze drifted from his broad shoulders to his narrow waist and perfect butt, strictly by reflex. I guiltily looked away, and felt the color rising in my cheeks.

This person had turned back to me now, the towel wrapped around his hips. He noticed my blush and grinned as he said, "Well, good. You must be feeling better if you're thinking about that." Oh God.

He came and stood right beside me. His proximity made my heart race. I dropped my gaze from his incredibly handsome face and noticed he was wearing a thick silver chain with a crucifix that rested right between his nipples. "I'm going to take a look at your injury and get a better bandage in place," he said as he pulled the wet rag off my head and knit his brows. He grabbed a clean hand towel and dabbed my forehead as I flinched.

"The first aid kit is—" I started to say, as he opened the third drawer and pulled it out. "You know its location how?"

"I've spent a lot of time in this house." He pulled a roll of gauze from the case.

"Are you an axe murdering stalker?" I was only sort of joking.

That got a smile from him, his face lighting up so beautifully that my breath caught. "Not exactly."

As he gently wrapped a bandage around my skull, I said, "You're as real as I am. And maybe I didn't actually go insane tonight, so that would make you, what? Nikolai's grandson? Or maybe his great grandson?"

He met my gaze. "That's good. Let's go with that." A smile still lingered on his full lips. He secured the bandage and then scooped me into his arms again. Pain shot up from my left leg and I sucked in my breath. "Sorry," he murmured.

"What's wrong with my leg?"

"I'm pretty sure you broke it." He carried me out of the bathroom and lay me gently on the unmade bed, then pushed my towel aside to uncover my leg and ran an assessing hand down its bruised and swollen length.

I propped myself up on my elbows and watched him. "I don't think it's broken. It would hurt more."

"The leg's started to heal, but it still has a long way to go." Carefully, clinically, he examined the rest of me, lifting each arm in turn, bending it carefully, and then running his big hands over my rib cage, my collar bone, my other leg. There were plenty of cuts and scrapes and bruises on my body, but none of the areas he touched were particularly tender.

He sat beside me on the bed, his hip against my rib cage. "I still can't believe you did that, getting drunk and running off into the woods. It was incredibly irresponsible." I looked away, ashamed at having done something so stupid. The stranger sitting beside me covered me with a blanket and turned off the light on the nightstand. Then he gently brushed my hair back from my bandaged forehead. "Promise me you won't ever do anything like that again," he said gravely.

"It wouldn't do any good to promise," I told him honestly. "I do a lot of stupid things." My eyelids were getting heavy, but I forced them open.

"Go to sleep, Nathaniel." He was still gently stroking my damp hair.

"No. I have too many questions. I need to know who you are, I need to know your name. I need to know how you found me and what you did to save me. I was really hurt. How am I getting better already?"

He pulled the red blanket toward my chin. "It would take too long to explain right now. You need to sleep."

I tried to sit up, stubborn even through my exhaustion. "No. I need to know what's going on." My body shuddered, letting go of some of the adrenaline that had coursed through me tonight.

He tried to gently push me down onto the pillow, but I resisted. So he sighed and came around to the other side of the bed, and climbed under the covers with me. He drew me into his arms, cradling me against his shoulder, and automatically I wound my arms around him and clung to him. Then I realized what I was doing and blinked in surprise. But I didn't let go of him. Because this felt completely wonderful.

And completely familiar.

"You've been here before. With me, like this," I said quietly. The realization made my heart jump. He didn't say anything. "I dream of someone that looks like you all the time. Were those…not dreams?"

Just the faintest hint of amusement crept into his voice. "In some cases, you really were dreaming. The sex dreams were all you, I had nothing to do with those." He shifted slightly, settling me against him. "Don't worry about it now. Go to sleep."

"But the other dreams," I persisted, even though sleep was weighing on me heavily, "the ones with you holding me like this…."

After a moment, he admitted, "That was real."

"Why did I think I'd dreamt it?"

He exhaled softly and said, "Because I manipulated you into forgetting it really happened."

"That's not possible." Sleep was pressing down hard. I fought against it.

"Sleep, Nathaniel." His words pushed me farther under somehow.

"No." It was barely a whisper, sleep closing fast. But there was something I needed to say, even through this fog. I forced myself upright, my exhausted body shaking with the effort. "I need you to be here in the morning. I need you to promise."

"I can't promise that."

"Promise!" A wave of dizziness crashed into me and I almost fell over. He captured me in his arms and pulled me onto his chest, and I clung to him with the last of my strength. I whispered, "Promise you'll stay, or I'll go back into the woods looking for you. Tomorrow night I'll go."

He swore in a foreign language, the intent clear even if I didn't understand the words. "Threatening your own safety is a very low tactic."

"You know I'll do it," I murmured. "Now promise you'll stay so I can go to sleep."

He sighed dramatically, then said, "I promise. I'll be here when you wake up."

I nodded, curling up against his chest, and let sleep take me.

Chapter Thirteen

It was past dawn. I'd managed to sleep in, but for how long I didn't know. I sat up carefully, my head pounding.

I pulled back the covers and looked at myself. My left leg was swollen, my body bruised and scraped. I stuffed some pillows behind my back to prop myself up and tried to sort out what had happened to me last night. It *was* only last night, wasn't it? It was all really confusing, fantasy and reality swirled together so thoroughly that I couldn't pick them apart. I tried to focus on what I knew.

There'd been the woods. And Nikolai. Or someone that looked exactly like him.

I'd been badly hurt. He fixed me somehow.

And he'd promised to stay. That I remembered clearly. He'd promised to stay, and yet I was alone.

"Damn it," I mumbled, draping an arm over my eyes. I knew I'd really been hurt, the signs of trauma were still all over my body. But I had to wonder how much of the rest of it had been some sort of delusion, or dream, or hallucination.

And apparently I was still hallucinating, because I thought I smelled coffee.

Some small sound caught my attention, and I sat bolt upright. The person that looked like Nikolai was coming up the stairs. He avoided the third step automatically – the one that squeaked. He was barefoot and dressed in the same dark t-shirt and jeans as last night, but now they were clean and dry. And he was carrying a white coffee mug.

"This is one elaborate hallucination," I said, my heart beating wildly. "You even knew to avoid the step that squeaks."

He came to stand beside me, and held out the mug. I fully expected it to dissolve in my grasp like a mirage, but it was heavy and warm to the touch. Very real. He glanced (guiltily?) back at the steps. "Oh. Yeah. Force of habit."

I took a sip of coffee, my eyes never leaving the person beside me, then said, "I have no idea which is worse: finding out I've gone insane, or finding out there really is a stalking doppelganger in my bedroom." He sat beside me on the bed, the mattress dipping beneath his weight. His pale blue eyes were locked on mine as he picked up my left hand without a glance or a moment's hesitation, a gesture as automatic as skipping the squeaking stair. I squeezed the big hand that held mine and said quietly, "What's your name?"

"Please don't ask me that. I don't want to have to lie to you."

"Just tell me the truth."

He broke my gaze, turning his face away from me. But he still held my hand.

I rolled over, partially onto his lap as I set the coffee on the nightstand, then pulled the drawer open and took out the tan cardboard folder. I leaned back against the pillows and set the folder in his lap as I said, "But you don't need to tell me your name, do you? Because I already know it."

"I wish you'd never found that photo," he said softly, still not looking at me.

"Why?"

"Because it hasn't been good for you." He picked up the folder with his free hand and placed it on the nightstand.

"It has." I couldn't begin to explain all that picture meant to me – I couldn't explain how or why it meant *everything*, why it was profoundly important to me somehow. And I certainly couldn't explain why I needed him to be the person in that photograph. Not just someone that looked like him. I *needed* him to be Nikolai.

"No." He met my gaze now. "It's hurt you. It sent you running out into the forest, chasing a ghost—"

"No, not a ghost."

He sighed. "Okay, not a ghost."

"That's a picture of you. Taken in 1927," I said, gesturing at the folder.

A long pause. And then a single word. "Yes."

"Nikolai." A whisper. A prayer.

"Yes."

Without logical thought – without any thought whatsoever – I launched myself at him, ignoring the pain shooting through my leg as I straddled him and grabbed his face between my hands and kissed him passionately, intensely, crying out against his lips.

And then his strong arms were around me, his hands nearly bruising me as he kissed me with a passion matching my own. He murmured, "Oh God, Nathaniel," before his tongue pushed into my mouth.

The towel had fallen away, so I was naked on his lap and could feel his erection straining against his jeans. I rubbed against it wantonly as his fingers laced in my hair, and then he tightened his grip, pulling my head back. He kissed his way down my neck and murmured against my skin, "Aren't you going to ask how that's possible? How I was in a photograph taken that long ago?"

"Yes. Later."

"Later?"

"After you fuck me."

"I'm not going to fuck you." He licked my earlobe and it sent a wave of desire down my spine. I jerked reflexively, then grunted as pain shot through my left leg.

"Why not?" I demanded, kissing his throat.

"Well for starters, because you're injured." He lightly ran his palm down my left leg.

"I don't care."

"But I do." He contradicted his gentle words by biting down on my shoulder, not hard enough to break the skin, but just barely. I cried out and bucked on his lap, and he grabbed my ass with both hands. "Nathaniel, sweetheart, we have to stop," he said before his mouth found mine again.

"We don't," I murmured against his lips as my shaking hands desperately tried to unfasten his belt.

"Baby, stop."

"No." I nipped his bottom lip as I struggled with the buckle.

In a move so quick and fluid that I barely knew what happened, he flipped me onto my back and straddled my hips, holding my wrists effortlessly against the mattress. His face was inches above mine, and when our eyes met I saw a dangerous, burning desire in their aquamarine depths.

It was more raw and more intense than anything I'd ever seen, and it made my heart race. It was wild. Animalistic. Completely feral. In that moment, I knew for a fact this man was dangerous. Maybe even deadly. But I didn't care. No, more than that. I *liked* it. Instead of frightening me away, it acted like gasoline on the fire raging within me, made my need for him explode exponentially, and I barely recognized my own voice when I rasped, "Nikolai, fuck me."

His voice was a low growl, lust and violence barely contained. "If I fuck you now, I'll hurt you."

"I don't care."

He threw his head back and yelled, and it was utterly inhuman. The powerful muscles in his arms and shoulders flexed, his hands crushing my wrists, and he bared his teeth as if he meant to rip my throat out. He looked into my eyes again, and I could see the battle raging within him. Bestial violence fought the last of his control, his body shaking from the effort of holding himself back, from what exactly I wasn't sure.

I should have been afraid. I should have been trying to get away. But instead, maybe because I was drunk with desire, or because I was absolutely reeling from the miracle of Nikolai's very existence, I just stared at him in amazement and murmured, "What are you?"

Whether that was the exact right thing to say, or the exact wrong thing I guess depends on your perspective. After a long moment he blinked, coming back to himself. He released my wrists and got off me, retreating to the far side of the room, staring at me as if *I* was the one that was dangerous.

He took a deep, shaking breath. Then another. It seemed as if he'd stopped breathing entirely when he'd been lost to his wild side.

I could see the debate raging within him, whether to stay or run from this room, from this house, from my life. I could read it so clearly in the tense lines of his body, the look in his incredibly expressive eyes. "Stay," I said softly.

He exhaled slowly. He was calm now, contained. The danger had passed. *Killer Elvis has left the building*, a crazy little part of my brain quipped.

And then he said, "At some point, you and I need to have a very long talk about your death wish."

"I don't have a death wish."

"You know I'm dangerous." It wasn't a question. It was a statement of fact. He crossed the room to me and perched on the edge of the mattress, then picked up my hands so he was again holding both my wrists, but gently this time. "I saw it in your eyes, the moment you figured it out. But you were absolutely unafraid, only aroused." His brows were drawn together and he frowned slightly, not in disapproval, but as if he was trying to make sense of me as his thumbs gently massaged my wrists.

"I know."

"And yet you want me to stay."

I nodded. He watched me for a long moment before letting go of me, then crossed the room to my duffle bag and pulled out a t-shirt and a pair of shorts, which he brought to me as he said, "Please get dressed, so I can stop thinking about fucking your brains out."

I knew better than to argue, and pulled the shirt on before asking lightly, noting the lack of underwear, "Does it do something for you if I go commando?"

"Yes." A little half-smile played on Nikolai's full lips. "I would have brought you some boxers anyway, but they're all in the dryer."

I raised myself up carefully, my left leg not willing to take my weight, and pulled the shorts on. "Meaning what? That you did my laundry?"

"My clothes were wet and dirty, so I put them in the washer after you fell asleep last night. There was a pile of your clothes in the laundry room, so I washed some of your things, too." Well, okay.

"Are you ever going to answer my question?" I asked as I finished getting dressed. "Are you going to tell me what you are?"

"No. At least...not yet. Come on, you should eat something," he said, changing the subject. He scooped me up like I weighed about as much as a dry towel and carried me downstairs, where he deposited me on the couch and went to the kitchen and started pulling random items from the refrigerator.

"What are you doing?"

"Making you breakfast." He rested his hands on his narrow hips, surveying the pile of ingredients before him.

"You don't need to do that," I told him.

"I do, actually. After all you did to yourself last night, you definitely need to eat."

"Okay. Then let me help you."

I started to get up from the couch, but he shot me a look and used a bunch of celery to point at me as he said, "Sit back down. I mean it. You're going to re-break your leg if you try to walk on it."

I rolled my eyes but sat back down, and he lined up the food on the counter and then shifted the order a couple times as if playing a shell game, like maybe rearranging the groceries might make a recipe magically appear before him. "Re-break?" I repeated. "That doesn't make any sense. If my leg was broken, how could it possibly have healed so fast?"

"Start with an easier question," he said, not looking up from the counter.

"Why do you look exactly the same now as you did in 1927?"

He met my gaze, grinning just a little. "Easier than that."

"Do you have any freaking idea how to cook?"

He smiled at that one. "Not really, no."

"Look, before you go through the trouble of making a—" I craned my neck to look at the counter, "celery, orange, chocolate syrup, lettuce omelet, can I offer a suggestion?"

"Yes."

"How about if you just bring me some cereal? It's in the cupboard to the left of the fridge. Yellow box. Dump it in a bowl. Pour milk on it. That's the white stuff that gets squeezed out of cows," I grinned.

He smirked at me, then did as I suggested. After he handed me the bowl of cereal, he sat down at the opposite end of the couch and carefully lifted my left leg to rest across both of his. "Thanks," I said and tucked into my breakfast, trying not to be self-conscious about the fact that he was watching me eat.

After a while, he said quietly, "I don't know why you're taking all of this so well. Not just what almost happened upstairs, but all of it." His hand was lightly caressing my bare foot, which he held in his lap.

"I don't either." I wiped my mouth with the back of my hand. "I should be completely freaked out right about now."

"Yes, you should."

"But instead, I'm confused as hell and in need of answers. For you to be here, the laws of nature, physics, logic, and common sense all have to be out of whack. You should have died years ago. Or at the very least, you should be as shriveled as Yoda by now. I just don't get it."

"I know."

I frowned at him. "It's really frustrating that you're not just telling me what's going on. I mean, what could possibly stop a person from aging? What would you have to be? A clone? A freak of nature? A genetic experiment, vampire, doppelganger, Dorian Gray or the recipient of shitloads of plastic surgery? Discoverer of the fountain of youth? A sorcerer? An alien? Should I keep guessing?"

"No, don't keep guessing."

"You really are Nikolai."

"Yes."

I raised an eyebrow and asked him, "Why aren't you telling me how this can possibly be happening?"

"I just…I can't."

I stared at him for a long moment. And then I said, "Fine. Tell me something else then."

"What?"

"Are you planning to stick around?"

"Definitely not."

Disappointment stung like acid in my mouth. "You're not?" I set the cereal bowl on the coffee table.

"No. I'm going just as soon as I know you're well enough to take care of yourself."

"Awesome." I looked away, staring out the window. The rain had stopped, and the lake sparkled in the sunlight.

"Nathaniel," he began.

"Nate. Everyone calls me Nate," I said, trying and failing to keep my voice emotionless.

"No love, you're most definitely Nathaniel." My name sounded like the auditory equivalent of a caress when he said it. "And I have to go. I think you know that as well as I do."

"Why? Because you're dangerous?"

"Yes."

"But Nikolai, I don't care." I held up my hand as he started to stay something and added, "But you do care. I get it. You're worried about hurting me. And for good reason. Whatever it is you're not telling me, I know it's bad. *But I don't fucking care.* I'm totally willing to take the risk, if it means getting to spend time with you. I'd give anything for that. I'd give *everything.*"

"Why? Why risk your life just to spend time with me? You don't even know me."

"You said that to me once before," I told him. "One of the nights I thought I was dreaming, you said exactly that. You came here and you held me, and you talked to me. Actually, you did more than that, didn't you? You picked me up off the kitchen floor, tucked me in bed, and then you stayed and comforted me."

He looked away.

I pressed harder. "That wasn't the only time, was it? There were lots of other times you came to me that I can barely remember."

His guilty expression was a perfectly clear yes.

"No wonder I feel so comfortable with you. We've spent a lot of time together, haven't we?" I paused and looked at him closely, then said, "How on earth did you make me forget all of that? And why did you keep coming here, Nikolai? You watched me, too – that feeling I kept having, it wasn't my imagination, it was *you*, wasn't it? Why were you watching me?"

Finally, he turned to meet my gaze. "The first day, it was just idle curiosity. I'd heard your vehicle and wondered who was at Rose's house, so I came to take a look. And God, you were – and are – so beautiful that I just stayed and watched you as you fell asleep out on the deck." His voice rose as he said, "And then you didn't wake up! It was twenty seven degrees that night. You would have frozen to death your first night here!" He was angry now.

"You did something to wake me up. You made some kind of noise," I guessed.

"I slammed two rocks together. If that hadn't woken you, I would have carried you inside."

"The fire, later that night...I couldn't get it going. But when I woke up, it was burning and the house was warm. Was that you, too?"

He nodded.

"So you kept coming back to keep an eye on me, because you realized I was far too stupid to look after myself," I said flatly.

"No! I kept coming back because I couldn't stay away from you."

"After saving me from freezing to death that first night, you must have felt some kind of responsibility to the poor idiot who didn't even know how to make a fire in a damn fireplace."

"Do you remember what else you did your first night here?" he asked, and I shrugged. "You ran around naked, trying to get a big moth out of the house. And while you were trying to get him to the door, you kept narrating what was happening like it was a badly dubbed Japanese monster movie. You kept calling him Mothra, and whenever he'd fly directly at you, you'd yell and dive behind the furniture." His eyes sparkled with amusement as I stared at him in open-mouthed horror. "It was the cutest thing I've ever seen," he told me.

I said, my voice tight with embarrassment, "I can only imagine what other ridiculous things you watched me do over those weeks. No wonder you kept coming around. I must have been funnier than a sitcom."

"That's in no way why I kept watching you."

"No, there was also the aforementioned need to make sure I didn't die of total stupidity."

He sighed and said, "I kept watching you because you're the most fascinating, charming, sweet, beautiful, and utterly adorable person I've ever seen in my entire life."

I frowned at him. We watched each other for a long moment, a range of emotions flickering through me as I tried to find the one that fit, and as I replayed all I'd been doing over the last few weeks that really shouldn't have had an audience. Then my eyes went wide and I exclaimed, "Fuck, Nikolai! The fucking *deer!*"

"What?"

"The deer! The ones that ran toward me when I yelled. Not *away*. The day—" my face heated up from the ferocity of my blush, "the day I masturbated on the deck. It's not that they were running *toward* me, it's that they were running *away* from you!"

"Oh." He looked embarrassed now, too. "Well, yes. Exactly. They had the sense to get the hell away from me, before I tore them all limb from limb."

"Why would you have done that?"

He met my gaze. "Because the sight of you pleasuring yourself was so arousing that I almost completely lost control."

I thought about the predator looking back at me from the depths of his pale blue eyes when we'd been up in the bedroom. And I told him levelly, "I need to know what you are."

"It doesn't matter. All you need to know is that I'm dangerous, and that's why I'm leaving as soon as you're well."

I kept watching him closely as I mentally replayed that day on the deck. Then I said, "There was a loud sound right before I went inside that day. What was that?"

Nikolai said quietly, "That was me snapping a tree in half as I tried to hold myself back."

"Back from what?"

"I'm not sure."

I wanted to keep talking about this, but my head was pounding and I was so tired. My body, after all I'd done to it last night, ached all over. The fatigue must have shown on my face, because without a word, Nikolai scooped me up and carried me upstairs, and crawled under the covers with me.

I put my arms around him, my head on his chest, and he held me securely. And after a while I said softly, "I don't care what you are. I just need you with me."

"Nathaniel—"

"I know what you're going to say. I know you're dangerous. The thing you're not telling me, the thing that keeps you from aging – I know it's bad. But you're not going to hurt me."

"What are you basing that on?"

"This. Right now. You've been close to me for several weeks, you've held me just like this many times. More than I know, right?"

He nodded.

"You're afraid you'll hurt me if you're close to me. But you've already *been* close to me, and I'm fine."

"I hadn't hurt you physically before today," he said, running his fingertips lightly over my bruised wrist, "But I *have* been hurting you. I invaded your privacy. I made you feel paranoid when I was watching you. I made you think you were going crazy, let you think you were talking to a ghost in your sleep. I let you keep that photo when I should have thrown it in the fire the night you found it. And I let you find the art studio, which I knew wouldn't be good for you. Though I never imagined you'd try to go there drunk in the middle of the night."

"You didn't *let me* find the studio. I found it on my own."

"I should have taken the key from you, after you became so fixated on that first photograph. I should have made sure you never went there."

"Yeah, yeah, it's all your fault. Be sure to blame yourself for being absolutely gorgeous, too, as long as you're trying to weed out the roots of my obsession."

"Nathaniel.…"

"Just don't go."

He wrapped his arms around me and stroked my hair gently. An interminably long moment passed. Finally, he said quietly, "I won't leave until you're fully recovered. I can't make any promises beyond that." Well, at least that would buy me more time to convince him to stick around. "Get some rest, Nathaniel. And when you wake up, I'll cook you some lunch."

I grinned at that. "I don't know about the idea of you cooking, Nikolai. That chocolate syrup-lettuce omelet you were contemplating earlier looked downright lethal." He chuckled as I curled up against him and let my eyes close.

Chapter Fourteen

When I awoke from my nap, I heard Nikolai doing something in the kitchen downstairs. Pots rattled, and then I heard a faint, "Ow! *Skata*!" Followed by the sound of something like apples hitting the floor.

"Oh dear God," I whispered under my breath, "What are you cooking?"

There should have been no way he heard that, but he called up to me, "It's supposed to be stew. I'm sorry I woke you."

I raised an eyebrow at his sonic hearing superpower, and tested it out again by saying, even more quietly, "By stew, do you mean you took everything from the refrigerator and put it in one big pot?"

I heard him laugh, and he called up to me, "Of course not. I found a cookbook. I may not know how to cook, but I do know how to read."

"Come get me," I said. "I want to see what you're doing." That was one notch below a whisper.

And here he came up the stairs, looking adorably rumpled, and dear God, wearing a red and white polka dot apron over his t-shirt and jeans. I burst out laughing.

He stood over me with his hands on his hips, smirking at my laughter. "Go ahead," he said, "get it out of your system."

"It's just so incongruous," I told him. "It's like someone sneaking into a museum and putting an apron on Michelangelo's David. Or, you know, whatever the Greek equivalent of David is. And that's what you are, right? Greek? Is that the language you lapse into when you swear?"

"Yes. Now do you want to come downstairs, or stay here and continue to laugh at me?"

I beamed at him. "I can laugh at you downstairs just as easily as I can here."

He grinned and scooped me up, not into his arms, but over his shoulder in a fireman's carry, and on the way downstairs he swatted my butt. Once he'd put me on one of the barstools at the counter, I took a look at the kitchen and exclaimed, "Holy shit! Was there some kind of industrial accident? Did the refrigerator explode?" Every available surface was piled with food, pots, pans, cutting boards, and pretty much every other thing in the kitchen that might potentially be a cooking implement.

"I'm sorry," he said. "I know it's bad. I promise to clean it up once I've finished."

"You could have just opened a can of soup if you were determined to make me lunch," I told him.

"I didn't want to feed you that crap."

"The canned stuff's not so bad. It's what I grew up on."

"You deserve better," he said simply. He'd gone to a far corner of the kitchen, where he was attempting to chop some vegetables.

"At least let me help," I said. "Bring that cutting board here. I can chop while I sit."

He did as I asked, setting the heavy wooden board down on the breakfast bar and handing me a knife. He leaned companionably against my right thigh as he picked up his own knife, knitting his dark brows as he concentrated on dicing, or trying to dice, a pepper. We shared the cutting board easily since I was left-handed, my knife on the opposite side of the board from his, and I went to work on the potatoes and onions before me.

I marveled at how comfortable I felt around Nikolai, and he seemed relaxed around me as well. There was an easy camaraderie between us that made it feel like we'd been doing this for ages. But then, we had known each other for several weeks…even if I couldn't remember most of it. And yeah, I seriously had questions

137

about that, about all of it. But I didn't want to push too hard right now and send him running.

Lunch turned into dinner as the preparations took over two hours. We kept the conversation light. I taught him what little I knew about cooking and entertained him with anecdotes about the white trash foods I'd grown up on (two words: sugar sandwiches. I mean really, who does that?)

Nikolai seemed to think I could conceivably starve to death in that two hour timeframe, so every time he passed by me in the kitchen, he popped something into my mouth – a bit of cheese, a strawberry, a slice of carrot. His concern for my well-being was so sweet, so genuine that I let him do it for a while, until I finally had to point out that at this rate, I'd be too full to eat the stew he was laboring over.

When it was almost dinnertime, I slid off the barstool and experimentally put a little weight on my leg. Across the kitchen, Nikolai turned and watched me closely, his brow creased with concern. The leg was stiff and achy, but I thought maybe it would hold me, so I took a little step forward. It collapsed under me as pain shot through my body, and I cried out as I fell.

But I didn't land on the floor. I landed in Nikolai's arms. Once the pain ebbed enough for me to catch my breath, I murmured, "So, incredible speed's definitely going on your list of superpowers, along with agelessness and sonic hearing." He looked a little alarmed as I met his gaze, so I added cheerfully, "And if you can fly, Superman, you have to promise to give me a ride."

He held me against his chest, and I kissed the exposed skin at his throat and felt a shiver of pleasure run through him. Then he said, "I want to do something that's going to seem completely bizarre, and I know asking you to trust me is a big request. But would you just go with it?"

I had no idea what I was agreeing to, but I nodded. And Nikolai reached up and grabbed a big knife that was on the counter.

Before I could say a word, Nikolai used the chef's knife to slice his finger open, then slid his fingertip between my lips. My eyes went wide as his blood filled my mouth. And then my lids slid shut and I moaned with pleasure, swallowing automatically. Warmth and nourishment flooded me as I suckled deeply, hungrily. The taste was lush, rich, wonderful.

Familiar.

I held his hand between both of mine and drank from him without conscious thought. In the next moment, I'd pushed him onto his back on the floor and climbed on top of him, kissing him deeply, then broke away for a moment and stared into his eyes. "Why did you do that?"

"How does your leg feel?"

I gasped and murmured, "You healed me," before claiming his mouth in another deep kiss. Then I whispered against his lips, "Is your blood also an aphrodisiac?"

"Apparently it is, if you drink enough of it." He grinned a little as his big hands ran up my back.

"What are you?" I asked again, but before he could answer, I shoved my tongue in his mouth, and he sucked it and moaned against my lips, cupping my ass as I ground my cock against his.

"If we don't stop, I think you're going to find out the hard way."

"I don't want to stop. I want to fuck you," I murmured as I licked and nibbled my way down his throat.

"Oh God." A shiver of desire ran through his body. But then he rolled over so I was underneath him and sat up. "I've been thinking, and maybe there's a way we could do that safely. But no way should we do this now. You're kind of…under the influence. We should wait until the effects of drinking from me wear off."

I ran my hands up his denim-clad thighs, then asked, "I'm guessing safe sex with you has a whole new meaning. We're talking about controlling the dangerous part of you, right?"

"Exactly." He brushed my hair back from my face so gently that it was hard to believe there was anything dangerous about him at all. "If you chained me, completely tied me down, you could fuck me. I couldn't hurt you then."

A tremor of desire went through me. "Where are we supposed to get chains?" I asked, my hands sliding up his broad back.

"I have some."

"You do? Why?"

His answer shocked me. "Because long ago, I was kept as a pleasure slave." For the first time, just a hint of vulnerability appeared in his eyes.

"Oh. Was it…was it consensual?" I wondered if maybe he was telling me he'd been in a dom/sub relationship, but I kind of didn't think so.

He shook his head no and climbed off me, kneeling beside me, and I sat up and gathered him into my arms. "Oh God," I whispered, holding him tightly. That had certainly sobered me right up.

"It's okay," he said, kissing my hair. "It was a long time ago. Don't let it upset you." He stood up then, pulling me to my feet with him, and changed the subject by saying, "Come on, dinner's ready. You need a good meal." I was so rattled by his revelation that I let him lead me to the breakfast bar and sat down without protest.

The stew, after the huge effort of making it, was absolutely delicious, nourishing and satisfying. I was ravenous and ate two big bowlfuls, which seemed to please Nikolai. He on the other hand ate almost nothing, just sampling a vegetable or two from the small bowl he'd gotten himself.

After dinner we moved to the couch, tangled up in each other, and I tasted his mouth as he parted his lips for me. Nikolai broke the kiss after a while, a tremor going through his body as he murmured, "God I fucking want you." His rock-hard cock was pressed firmly against my own, and he thrust his hips slightly, rubbing against me.

"Same here."

He said, his voice a bit rough, "Would you like me to get the chains?"

"Are you sure you want to let yourself get chained up?"

"I trust you, Nathaniel, and I need you in me. Please," he whispered, intense longing in his eyes.

"Yes. God yes," I murmured before kissing him again.

He rolled off me so he was standing beside the couch and took a deep breath. "It'll just take me a couple minutes to go get them. Meet you in the bedroom." I nodded and he smiled shyly before leaving the lake house at a jog.

I took the stairs to the loft two at a time – my leg was perfect now and I felt strong, maybe better than I ever had. I pulled my clothes off as I crossed the room to the big bed and pushed the comforter aside with shaking hands.

Soon Nikolai was back, dropping a bunch of chains on the floor with a clatter as he set a little glass jar and a set of keys on the nightstand. His big hands encircled my waist from behind, and he buried his face in my hair. A low growl rumbled in his throat.

I turned to face him. Nikolai had to be about six-three, he had a good five inches on me, and so much more muscle mass. And burning in his eyes right now was raw danger, that wild intensity I'd caught of a glimpse of before. It would have been unnerving, but in the next moment Nikolai got on his knees before me and looked up at me. And he said in a low voice, "Just stay in control, Nathaniel."

"I'm not in danger of losing control."

"I mean, stay in control of me. Tell me what to do, teach me to obey you."

"Oh." I got it now, I got how this could work. If whatever lived under his skin was held in check, we could do this. A bit of self-doubt crept in. Did I even have an inner dominant? Would I be able to pull this off? But I wanted Nikolai more than I'd ever wanted anything in my life, and if this was what it took to have sex with him, I was damn well going to man up and learn to take control. I kept my voice firm and level as I said, "Take your clothes off, Nikolai."

He obeyed instantly, pulling off his t-shirt and then the heavy chain and crucifix around his neck before shucking his jeans. He was barefoot and wore no underwear, which meant that he was now completely naked and looking up at me in anticipation. I bent over and kissed him and he parted his lips for me, and claimed his mouth with my tongue.

When I straightened up, he locked eyes with me and slowly ran the tip of his tongue up my achingly hard cock. This was slightly unsettling, because the look in his eyes when he did that was completely predatory.

I stepped back and held my voice steady as I told him, "Lay out the chains on the bed." He obeyed instantly.

It was an illusion, the idea that I could control him. He was so much bigger, his powerful body probably even stronger than his solid, well-defined muscles suggested. But domination didn't really have anything to do with physical strength, I realized. It had to do with mindset. The obvious circus-tiger-and-trainer analogy came to mind. Clichéd, but apt.

After pushing all the blankets and pillows off the far side of the bed, he ran the chain from a pair of heavy shackles through the iron headboard. He had two more sets of restraints, each comprised of two wide cuffs separated by a couple feet of chain, and fastened one cuff from each of these to the bars of the headboard as well.

Nikolai got on his back on the mattress and raised his arms over his head, laying his wrists in the open manacles. He maintained eye contact with me as a tremor shook his body, his powerful muscles flexing as he struggled to hold himself in check. And then he rocked back, bringing his knees to his shoulders, and spread his legs wide for me. A drop of precum glistened tantalizingly on the tip of his thick, hard cock, and my own cock throbbed at the sight of that.

Quickly, I climbed up onto the mattress and clicked the cuffs onto his wrists, then clamped the remaining restraints to each ankle. And as soon as I did that, Nikolai let out his breath, his body relaxing.

I leaned in and kissed him and he parted his lips for me. Then I asked, "Are you secure?"

He tensed his shoulders, wrapped his hands around the chain that connected his wrists, and pulled both hands up, hard. The heavy bed creaked and shifted a bit from the force of his pull, but the chains held. He looked up at me with a devilish grin and nodded.

I was so completely aroused that my hands shook as I grabbed the little glass pot on the nightstand. "Is this lube?" I asked him, and again he answered with a nod. I grinned at his foresight, then climbed between his spread legs and unscrewed the lid to the little jar, scooping up a dollop of thick, translucent cream with one finger. Though almost desperate in my need to fuck him, I was going to make sure he was prepped properly. I took a deep breath and slowly pushed one finger into his tight little opening.

He wasn't nearly as patient as I was. "You don't need to be gentle," he ground out, his voice pure gravel, writhing underneath me, trying to push himself down onto my hand. "Just take me." He bucked again, impaling himself hard, but I kept working him with my fingers, first one, and then a second until I felt him open up and knew he was ready for me.

"Damn it," I muttered, suddenly realizing something. "We need condoms. I haven't got any."

"Don't need them."

"We don't?"

He shook his head no. "I swear it."

I rubbed the thick, slippery cream over my shaft and pressed the swollen head of my cock against his opening. When I paused, trying to calm down enough so I didn't cum the moment I was inside him, Nikolai growled in frustration, pulling against the chains that bound his hands and feet. I pushed against him, my hands on his waist, and met with resistance for a moment. But then the resistance gave way, and I slid into him.

I meant to go slowly, to give him time to adjust. But he had just enough slack in his chains to meet my thrusts with his own, driving himself onto me again and again until he'd taken me to the hilt. I was lost to it then, finding a deep rhythm in him, his tight hole milking my cock, my balls pushing against his body on every thrust. It was my first time inside a man, and it was perfect ecstasy.

He rocked beneath me, his own rhythm urgent, then jerked wildly against his chains, a growl vibrating in his throat as he really tried to break free of his bonds. "Oh God, Nikolai," I moaned, falling forward as I took him, my head beside his. He bit down on my shoulder, hard, his teeth tearing my skin, and I gasped with surprise. Another growl rumbled through him, and then he moaned with pleasure.

He was drinking from me.

And it was the most erotic thing I could ever imagine, enough to push me right over the edge. My orgasm tore from my body as I thrust violently, yelling as I pumped into him. And that set him off too, his cock pressed between our bodies, his cum spraying both of us. He released my shoulder as he cried out.

I collapsed on top of him when my orgasm finally ebbed, kissing his face, his hair, wrapping my arms around him as I gasped for breath, my body shaking. When I could speak again, I pushed myself up onto my elbows and met his gaze. "I just knew you were a vampire," I told him. "But I didn't want to say it out loud, just in case I was wrong and you thought I was nuts." He watched me closely, his expression grave. I settled onto his chest, grinning widely, and murmured, "That's so fucking hot."

Chapter Fifteen

It was quite a while before he came back to himself enough to actually speak. I had unchained him, gotten a wash cloth from the bathroom and cleaned us up, then pulled the blanket over us and snuggled against him. He took me in his arms and held me, and when he finally spoke, what he said was, "How is that hot?"

"It just *is*. Way hotter than finding out you're a clone or an alien." I grinned and snuggled against him and kissed the side of his throat.

"I should have had you gag me too, so I couldn't bite you. Now we know for next time."

A wave of pleasure washed through me at the idea of a next time. I told him, "I actually loved it when you bit me."

"You did?"

"Absolutely. Any time you want to bite me during sex, feel free."

"Don't encourage it, Nathaniel. We got lucky. I could have easily lost control."

"But you didn't."

"Not this time."

I changed the subject by saying, "I'm sorry I didn't think of condoms sooner. Are you sure we didn't need them?"

"I'm not susceptible to human diseases, but even if I was, you're perfectly healthy."

"How do you know that about me?"

"If anything was off within you, I would smell and taste it."

"Well, good."

We spent a long time with me twined around him, unwilling to break the contact between us. Eventually I brushed the hair back from his forehead and said, "I kind of did a half-assed job cleaning us up. Do you want to take a bath with me?"

"That sounds wonderful."

We soaked together in the tub, gently kissing and washing and caressing each other. But our kisses soon became insistent, hungry. "I suppose," I whispered against his lips, "the fact that I'm not tired is because I drank from you earlier. Right?"

"Mmhmm." He was licking the little hollow beneath my left earlobe as his cock slid against mine.

"And are you sore from…you know…what we did earlier?"

He pulled back a bit and grinned at me. "Are you asking if I'm too sore for you to fuck me again?"

I smiled embarrassedly. "Yeah. That."

"I will never, ever be too sore for you to fuck me."

I ran into the bedroom to grab a couple things, leaving a wet trail there and back. I ended up bending him over right there in the bath, hooking his wrists to a leg of the heavy iron tub with the short chain and quickly working a bit of lube into him. We got on our knees inside the tub and I took him from behind, water halfway up our thighs, driving my cock into him again and again as we both bucked and moaned. I reached around him and grabbed his cock, pumping his shaft, bringing him to orgasm a moment before I poured myself into him.

Again it took a while for him to come back to himself. He didn't speak as I unchained him, and after I dried him off, we returned to bed. He pulled the red blanket over us, relaxing in my arms.

We were almost asleep when he gasped and sat up quickly.

"Nikolai, what is it?"

"My necklace. God, I almost forgot about it. Where is it?"

I jumped up and retrieved it from the floor, and slid it over his head. He winced as the heavy crucifix landed against his bare chest, but then he sighed and settled into my arms and shut his eyes.

"Is that a bad thing to forget?"

"Considering we're sleeping in a glass house, yes, it would be a very bad thing to forget. It's the only thing that keeps me from burning to death in the sun."

"Oh." That detail, that bit of mythology about burning in the sun, finally drove it home for me somehow. "You really are a vampire," I said quietly.

His eyes were open now, watching me closely.

Even if my sex-addled brain had sort of glossed over the complete bizarreness of the whole 'vampires are real' revelation, I *had* accepted it as fact. I apparently just hadn't given much thought to what it meant. I stared at him, trying to see him as a monster, as something deadly. But all I saw was my sweet, beautiful Nikolai.

"Chain me," he said quietly, "while you sleep. Or ask me to leave. Do whatever it takes to make yourself feel safe."

I caressed his cheek. "I do feel safe with you, Nikolai."

"I can see the fact that I'm a monster is just starting to sink in, though. You don't have to feel uneasy. And you don't have to keep me in your bed." His voice was so soft, his eyes pools of heartbreak even as he tried to keep his expression neutral.

I wrapped my arms around him and pulled him close. "I want you with me, and not just tonight. I don't want you to take off now that I'm healed."

"I shouldn't stay with you. I should go someplace far away."

"Is that what you want?"

"No. God no. I want to stay with you more than anything, even though that's incredibly selfish of me, even though I'm a danger to you. But I want you so much, Nathaniel."

I kissed his chest. "Good. Then it's decided."

"It is?"

"Yup. We both want this, Nikolai. We want to be together. So you're staying, and we're going to figure out how to make this work."

Chapter Sixteen

Over a week had passed since the first time Nikolai and I slept together, and we'd spent every day together since then. Despite our newfound intimacy, he'd shied away from all my questions at first, reluctant to talk about his past or to talk about himself much at all. But he was beginning to open up, revealing little bits and pieces about his life.

He held back in other ways as well. Whenever we had sex, he always insisted on the chains, only relaxing once he was tied down, and even then, only slightly. He was careful not to bite me again, clearly worried about losing control of the vampire side of him. He didn't trust himself, didn't trust his ability to keep the monster in check.

One morning as sunlight streamed into the lake house, the faint sounds of some sort of activity in the kitchen drifted up to me as I awoke. "What are you cooking this time?" I asked with a grin, stretching in bed and rubbing the sleep from my eyes. He'd developed an avid interest in preparing meals (which only I ate, of course), gradually working his way through Rose's cookbook.

Nikolai came up the stairs, dressed only in jeans and carrying a coffee mug, the heavy crucifix around his neck hanging between his well-defined pectorals. God, he was gorgeous. He grinned at me shyly as he handed me the mug and sat on the edge of the mattress.

"Good morning, sunshine. Thanks for the coffee," I said as I took the cup, then leaned forward and kissed his full lips. "You know, you can take a break from all the cooking if you want. You don't have to keep feeding me."

"I like taking care of you," he said, his voice subdued. "Breakfast will be ready in a few minutes. I tried to make quiche, it's in the oven. The crust is going to be inedible, but the filling might be alright." There was something about him this morning, an air of uncertainly, vulnerability in his eyes.

I set the coffee mug on the nightstand and straddled his lap, hugging him to me. "Are you okay?" I asked as he kissed my bare shoulder.

After a pause he said quietly, "I need to go out and hunt today." He took a deep breath. "I'd been putting it off for days, but I'm so hungry. I have to go. And it really scares me, because after I feed, I don't think you'll be safe around me."

"So, you're going to drink from a human."

"Yes."

"Are you…" I took a deep breath, "are you going to kill them?"

"No. I mean, probably not. When I start drinking deeply, it's easy to take too much, but these days I know when to stop." He didn't meet my eyes. "That hasn't always been the case. I've killed before, though the last time was decades ago. Now I have better control."

I processed that for a long moment, the fact that he'd killed. Some part of me had already come to terms with the fact that a vampire would probably have taken lives. And now that it was confirmed, I did that only thing I could: I dealt with it.

"I'm worried about what's going to happen afterward, after I've totally reverted to my vampire side and drunk my fill," he said. "It's always a long, slow process to take back control from him. The vampire is going to be so strong after he's fed, and he might come after you. Now that he has a mate, he might come looking for you."

"To do what to me?"

"To fuck you, to drink from you…I'm not sure. I've never had a mate before. But I can see him wanting you, needing you after he's fed." Nikolai's head was bowed, his black hair hanging in front of his eyes.

"Oh."

"I'm so sorry, Nathaniel. You shouldn't have to deal with any of this. You shouldn't have to deal with...me."

I hugged him tightly. "It'll be okay. We'll figure this out." He didn't say anything. "When do you...hunt?" I asked, trying to keep my tone neutral.

"After dark."

"So we have all day to come up with a plan to keep me safe."

The timer sounded from downstairs and Nikolai nodded as I swung off his lap. My beautiful, deadly vampire lover went to check on, of all things, the quiche he'd made me for breakfast. God, my life was weird.

*****

Around midday, I went for a long run while Nikolai worked on another elaborate recipe from Rose's cookbook. When I got back to the house, he was wearing a different outfit – a long-sleeved black button-down and faded Levis. So he'd obviously gone home at some point.

"You changed," I noted, coming around the counter to peer at the dough that sat before him and kissing his cheek.

"I had a bit of an accident with the mixer." He grinned ruefully. "Turns out you shouldn't add stuff to it while it's running on high."

"You know," I said as I brushed my sweat-dampened hair from my face, "You still haven't shown me where you live." He told me that he lived in the basement of Rose's old Victorian, which he'd moved into after the house burned down. But he'd been reluctant to take me there for some reason.

He looked up from the cookbook. "I can show you after lunch if you want."

"I'd like that." I got myself a glass of water, then ventured, "Can I ask you a question?"

"Sure."

"Were you and Rose Azzetti lovers?" I'd been curious about their relationship for a long time, and right now it seemed like he was in a talking mood.

"No."

"No?"

"She wanted us to be, but I couldn't give her what she wanted. I never had the desire to be sexually involved with a woman, and even if I had, it could never have worked out between Rose and me."

"So what were you to each other?"

"She was my best friend. And I guess I was her muse, among other things. She spent hours drawing me, painting me." He looked desolate as he said, "She was in love with me."

I sat on the counter, close to Nikolai. "Did she know what you are?"

"No. She suspected something was odd about me, of course. But in the three years we were friends, I kept the truth hidden from her."

"What happened between the two of you?"

"Eventually, I saw how her love for me was affecting her life. She moved out here full-time to be with me. She cut herself off from other people. She'd had a boyfriend, but she broke it off with him. I didn't want her to end up alone because of me. So after a while, I told her I was leaving, that we couldn't be together anymore."

"Where did you go?"

"Nowhere. She was still here all by herself, she wouldn't move back to town. I worried about her, worried that something would happen to her, that she'd get hurt or sick and need help.

I watched over her the last sixty years of her life."

"Without her knowing?" I asked incredulously.

"That's right."

"She must have known, though. I certainly felt it when you were watching me."

"I didn't watch her like that. I just remained within a mile or two of her, close enough to hear her if she was in distress."

"So she stayed at the lake even after she thought you left."

He sighed quietly. "Partly, she was waiting for me to come back. She never lost hope that maybe someday I'd change my mind and return to her. More than that, though, she came to love it here. This was her home. She learned to thrive in the isolation."

"Did she die here at the house?"

"No. When her health started to deteriorate at the end of her life, I placed an anonymous call to her sister in New Jersey, your stepdad's mother. The sister and her family came and got Rose and took her to a hospital on the coast." He looked up at me. "I visited her in the hospital, right before she died. I just…I wanted to say goodbye. I hadn't changed at all over the course of her life, so she thought she was dreaming when she saw me. But she was so happy. She held my hand and told me she loved me. Rose was holding my hand when she died."

"I'm sorry, Nikolai. That must have been so hard."

He turned his head and stared out at the lake for a while before saying quietly, "I wish I could have stayed with her throughout her life, it was wonderful to have a friend. But being with me was just so detrimental to her. She became infatuated with me. You know, you saw her studio." He kept staring out at the water. "I loved Rose so much. Not the way she needed me to, but I did love her."

"Why did you stay here, after she passed away?"

He shrugged. "I didn't have anywhere else to go. Besides, the basement of the old Victorian has been a good home for me, I like it there. You'll see why after lunch." Nikolai turned from me and went back to cooking. Subject closed, apparently.

*****

After I'd showered and eaten, we walked hand in hand through the woods. When we emerged into the clearing, he led me around to the far side of the old house's foundation. There was nothing remarkable about the part of the foundation where he stopped, but he slid his fingertips under a section of old flooring and raised a hidden panel. A wooden staircase descended into darkness.

"Go ahead," he said. "It's going to get very dark when I replace this hatch, but I'll be with you."

I climbed down the rickety staircase, and once I reached solid ground I took a couple steps back. He was right about it being dark. When the panel was put back in place, the darkness was absolute. I felt him right beside me, when a moment ago he'd been at the top of the stairs. "I'm going to pick you up, Nathaniel."

And then his arms were around me, strong and secure, lifting me up against his chest. He walked confidently through the blackness. "Can you actually see where you're going?"

"Yes, I can see perfectly. We're almost there, then I'll put some lights on for you."

I felt him duck down slightly, and then got the impression we'd entered a larger space. The air was still and cool, and he set me down on what had to be his bed.

A match was struck, his beautiful profile illuminated, and he brought the flame to an oil lamp. Golden light flared as the wick caught. He worked his way around the room, lighting several more lamps, bathing the space in a soft glow.

"Why do you have lamps if you can see in the dark?" I asked idly.

"Because they make it seem kind of cozy down here."

I grinned at that, a vampire calling something *cozy*, and then I looked around. The room was smaller than I'd anticipated. It held a narrow bed that was inset into a little alcove, a chair and desk, and an armoire opened to reveal a few clothes. And it was lined with books. There were hundreds of them on the shelves that covered three of the four walls floor to ceiling. "I suppose you've read all of those."

Nikolai smiled at me. He was kneeling a couple feet in front of me, watching me closely. And he said quietly, "Many, many times."

"Where'd they all come from?"

"Different places. I'm a bit of a scavenger, I find things people leave behind. Also, Rose knew I loved books, so she gave me quite a few of them. She enjoyed reading, but never read a book more than once. So when she met me, she gave me her entire collection, and then kept adding to it during the time we were friends."

I turned to look at the stone wall behind me. On it hung a beautiful watercolor of our lake. "Did Rose paint that?"

"Yes. She had an incredible gift, just like you do."

I grinned embarrassedly, then pivoted to look behind me in the other direction. And my eyes went wide. A thick metal ring was embedded in the stone wall above the headboard of the little bed. And attached to it where chains, thicker even than the heavy shackles we kept at the lake house. "Why are these here, Nikolai?"

"Because I've always thought I might need them one day, I might start to lose control of my vampire side. I wanted to have a way to restrain myself, just in case."

"But how would you get free after you'd regained control?"

"I wouldn't."

"So…you thought you might have to chain yourself up and let yourself die here?"

He looked at the stone floor. "I wouldn't die, I'd just go dormant after a while. If we're smart, we'll use those chains on me today and leave me here," he said softly. "You can take a lantern so you can find the stairs. The hatch isn't that hard to lift, so you can let yourself back out—"

"Why would we do that?"

"So I can't hurt you. If I end up killing you tonight when I'm wild and blood-drunk, I'll kill myself too, so I'm done for either way. But God, I don't want to take you with me."

"No way are we doing that! We'll figure something else out. At the very least, I can get in my car and go to town for a few days until things settle down, until it's safe to come back. Because no fucking way am I going to chain you up and leave you here to starve."

Nikolai looked at his hands, which were splayed across his thighs. "I could track you in town. I could track you anywhere. There's absolutely no place you could go that I couldn't find you."

"Still, chaining you up until you die – or go dormant, like that's okay somehow: *not an option*. So what else have you got?"

"I don't know."

"Didn't you ever try to come after Rose when you were feeding? What did you do to keep her safe?"

"I had no problem staying away from her. The reason you're in danger isn't because I consider you a food source. It's because my vampire considers you his mate now that we've had sex. It'll be the urge to fuck that sends him after you, far more than the urge to feed...though I suppose the desire to drink from his mate will call him, as well." *Mate*. What an odd term.

I told him, "Like I said, we'll figure something out." He nodded in agreement but didn't look convinced.

I pushed my Converse off my feet and reclined on his bed. The quilt was well-worn to the point of being silky with age, and his pleasant scent perfumed the pillow. Being in his bed was almost as good as being in his arms, it felt like an extension of him. I let my eyes slide shut for just a moment, savoring my surroundings, and Nikolai said softly, "I'll let you sleep if you want."

"I'm not napping, I'm just enjoying being in your bed. All that's missing is you. Come join me." I slid as far back as I could on the narrow mattress, my back meeting the cold stone wall. He must have known just how cold that wall was, because when he slid into bed with me he pulled me away from it, up on top of him. My full weight rested on him and I asked, "Would you tell me if I was crushing you?"

"No," he said with a little grin. "But you're not heavy at all."

My lips found his, and we spent a long time kissing. My hard cock pressed insistently into my belly – and his, since I was lying right on top of him. After a while he whispered, "You know you can take me if you want to. You can use the chains on the wall to restrain me. They do have keys, they're across the room in the armoire."

Soon he was on his stomach, the heavy cuffs around his wrists. I pulled his jeans down to mid-thigh and freed my straining cock from my shorts with one hand while I reached for a little pot of lube.

"Don't take this question the wrong way, Nicky," I grinned as I quickly worked the thick cream down my shaft, "but why do you have several containers of lube beside your bed?"

He grinned embarrassedly at me over his shoulder and admitted, "I, um, sometimes finger myself while I stroke my cock." A shiver of desire shot through me and I pushed two slicked fingers inside him, working him open. He was relaxed, ready for me, and I slid my length into his body.

We fucked hard and fast. I thrust into him again and again and he matched his own backward thrusts to mine, driving me in deeper. His legs were free so he came up onto his knees in a low crouch, and drove himself almost brutally back onto my cock. I moaned as he cried out under me and then I was emptying into him, yelling so loudly it might have caved the roof in.

He hadn't quite finished, so I pulled out of him and rolled him onto his side so I could take his cock in my mouth, and reached behind him and fingered his hole as I sucked him. "Oh God Nate, I'm gonna cum," he ground out. He started to pull out of my mouth but I held him in place with my free hand on his ass, sucking his thick cock until he yelled and shot into the back of my throat. I swallowed him down, moaning with pleasure.

"So that," I joked afterwards, as I eased my fingers out of him carefully, "is what it takes to get you to call me Nate."

He chuckled at that. His arms were stretched above his head, still chained, and he was relaxed, blissful. "I was in a hurry. I had to tell you I was going to cum, in case you didn't want to swallow. It would have taken too long to say your full name."

I started to climb over him to get the keys to unchain him, but he stopped me. "Wait. Will you please leave me chained up? Just for a few more minutes?"

"Sure. Why though?" I cleaned us both up a bit with a nearby cloth, then rested my head on his shoulder, my fingertips tracing the curve of his rib cage.

"It just feels good, knowing I can't hurt you. It means I can relax."

"Okay, if that's what you want. But there's no sign of your inner predator right now."

"He's always there, though," he said quietly. "I'm constantly worried about him when I'm with you."

"When the vampire takes over, where do you go? This part of you, I mean, my Nicky. Are you just gone? Or do you look out through his eyes and see what he's doing?"

He was quiet for a few moments before saying, "I'm not gone. Not really. I talk about the monster like he's separate from me, but he's really not. It isn't like Jekyll and Hyde, I don't wake up with blood on my lips and wonder where it came from. I know what he's doing.

It's just that, when I'm in the grip of bloodlust…I don't care. I have no sympathy, no compassion, no humanity when he takes over. I just become my hunger and it consumes me."

"The people you drink from, do they remember afterwards? Do they know what happened to them?"

"No. I compel them beforehand, so they're left with no memory of it."

"What does that mean, to compel someone?"

"Vampires have the power to influence others and to adjust their memories, so the people we feed from don't remember us. I know it sounds terrible, but it ensures the survival of our species, it keeps us hidden. Without it, we would have been hunted to extinction long ago."

"Did you compel me on those nights when you held me in your arms, and the next day I thought it was a dream?"

He nodded, looking guilty. "I know how wrong it was, manipulating you like that. I'm so sorry."

"I know I should be pissed about that, but I'm actually not. I absolutely loved those dreams, which is what I thought they were. But why'd you do it?"

"Because I longed to touch you, to be near you. I never imagined there was any way we could actually be together, so I didn't want you to know I was real, I didn't want you to get attached like Rose had, only to have to end it when it proved impossible." He said softly, "I never dreamt we could have this. But what I did was wrong, and I really am sorry."

"I know you are, Nicky." I kissed him gently. Then I asked, "I'm curious, are there a lot of vampires?"

"I don't know for sure, but I don't think so. There was a time when we were fairly plentiful, but it's been decades since I came across another of my kind. Not that I come across that many people, but still."

Since he was so receptive to answering questions today, I decided to ask another. "How old are you, Nikolai?" That was something I'd wondered for a long time.

"I don't know, actually. I've been like this for centuries, but I can't even give you a rough estimate. I have no memory of being human, so I don't know when I was born. I don't even remember my last name."

"What's your earliest memory?"

"Fighting. I was made to be a warrior, turned into what I am by a powerful vampire who wanted his own army. Eventually that vampire was killed," he said. "After that, his second in command imprisoned all of my maker's soldiers and kept us locked up for centuries, just in case he himself needed an army someday. The world was a very different place when I finally left that prison, but I have no idea how much time passed."

"How did you escape?"

"I didn't. I was taken from prison by a vampire who'd been my jailer. He decided to leave Russia, which is where we were being kept, and since he'd taken a liking to me he decided to keep me as a pleasure slave. He kept me in chains most of the time, but at least I was out of my cell."

I tightened my grip around him and kissed his forehead. The thought of Nikolai being enslaved tore my heart out. He said softly, "It's okay, Nathaniel. That part of my life ended more than a century ago."

I clung to him tightly as I asked, "What happened to that man?"

"My master was killed. He'd brought me to San Francisco in the late eighteen hundreds, thinking he'd be safe in the new world. But even here there were vampire hunters, and eventually one got to him. After his death, I took his necklace, the one that let him walk in sunlight, and packed up a few of his things along with the chains and travelled north."

He continued, "I wanted to get away from heavily populated areas. I'd never had to regulate my own hunger before, I was always fed by those that owned me. Once it was up to me to feed myself, I didn't trust myself around a lot of people. After drifting around the Pacific Northwest for a while, I eventually settled here around 1900, in an old fur trapper's cabin on the other side of the lake."

"We can't chain you up any more, Nikolai," I told him. "I can't hurt you like others hurt you." I swung out of bed and found the keys in the armoire and unfastened his cuffs, then laid back down with him.

He wrapped his arms around me and said, "It's in no way the same, Nathaniel. I love being chained when I'm with you, it's actually comforting. I like that the chains take control away from me so I don't have to worry so much about what I'll do. And it's more than that, too," he added quietly. "The chains make me feel like I belong to you. I love that feeling."

I kissed him gently, and we held each other for a while, snug in Nikolai's little bed. Eventually he said, "I think I just figured out what I need to do to keep you safe tonight."

I propped myself up on one elbow and looked down at him. He was so incredibly beautiful, luminous in the soft lantern light. I ran my hand down the side of his face as he said, "I can leave right after sundown, and I won't take my necklace. I'll spend all night travelling as far from you as possible, and I won't feed until close to dawn. At sunrise I'll have no choice but to seek shelter for the day, and it'll take all of the next night to return here. That should be more than enough time to regain control."

"Won't it be dangerous, having to seek shelter someplace unfamiliar? What if you can't find a place to stay before the sun starts to rise?"

"It'll be fine. I can always bury myself if nothing else."

"Bury yourself! But you'd suffocate!"

"I breathe out of habit, not out of necessity. I wouldn't suffocate."

I blurted, "There must be something else, something we can do that won't result in you having to bury yourself alive!" It was one of the most horrifying things I could imagine.

"It's not so bad. And I'm not actually burying myself *alive*...."

"Because you're—" I couldn't even say it.

176

"Not alive. Not technically."

I couldn't even sort of process that as I stared at him. Looking back at me was a thinking, feeling, caring person, clearly alive in every possible way. I shook my head and then rested it against his chest. "I don't really believe that." After a pause, during which I totally failed to get my head around the 'not alive' concept, I said, "I guess that's a good plan though, but I want you to try to end up someplace where you're sure you can find shelter. Burying yourself is just too terrible to contemplate."

Chapter Seventeen

Shortly before sunset that night, Nikolai and I were out on the deck of the lake house. I was on his lap, straddling him, my fingers tangled in his dark hair. We'd been kissing for who knows how long and there was an urgency to his kisses, tension in his body. "Nicky, are you worried you won't be coming back?" I asked him.

He nodded gravely. "Whenever I feed, there's a chance I could be killed. I get so focused on the blood that I become pretty unaware of my surroundings. It would be so easy for someone to come along and end me while I'm feeding."

"Oh God."

"I should have been taught to hunt and to control my bloodlust. No one ever showed me how. But despite that, I've managed to survive on my own for more than a century. I have every intention of coming back to you, and not as a blood-drunk monster. I also have every intention of keeping whoever I feed from alive."

"Are you sure you shouldn't just drink from me?"

He shook his head. "I'd probably lose control, because my desire for you is so incredibly intense and because I'm so hungry right now. I fear I'd tear you apart."

The sun had set by now, and Nikolai pulled the necklace over his head. I held my hand out, and he pooled the chain and the crucifix in my palm. "How does this keep you safe?" I asked.

"It was bespelled by a witch centuries ago to shield against the sun's deadly light. And I'm sure it wasn't done willingly."

"What makes you say that?"

"Because of what she chose to bespell. It could have been anything, it could have just been the chain itself. But instead she bespelled the crucifix, an object that doesn't rest easily against a vampire's skin."

"What do you mean?"

"It aches, all the time, a constant 'fuck you' from the person who bespelled it."

"Oh God."

"Yeah, exactly." He grinned and stood up then, easily swinging me around and depositing me on the lounge chair. "I need to get going. The sooner I start, the farther I can get from you before sunrise."

He unbuttoned his shirt and took it off, laying it over the back of the chair. I raised an eyebrow at that, and he explained, "I don't have a lot of clothes and this'll get torn up if I wear it. It's not like I pay any attention to running through thorns and brambles when I become the hunter." I was glad to see the jeans stayed on.

He took a step backwards, away from me, and said, "Take care of yourself, Nathaniel. I'll see you in about a day."

"Wait!" I leapt from the lounge chair and launched myself into his arms. He scooped me up effortlessly to make up for our height difference, and I wrapped my legs around him as I kissed him almost desperately. Finally I said, "Keep yourself safe, Nicky. I need you to come back to me."

"I promise I'll try my best to stay alive." He kissed me again and set me down before exhaling slowly. Then he turned and stepped off the deck.

I watched him go, illuminated in the light spilling from the lake house. He was barefoot, hands in his pockets, shoulders slumped. He got to the edge of the forest and looked back at me, and we held each other's gaze for a long moment.

Nikolai turned toward the woods then, and a subtle change came over him. He straightened up, squaring his shoulders. His hands, now at his sides, flexed slightly. It was as if strength was pouring into him, realigning his body, transforming him subtly into something different. Something more.

Abruptly, he took off running. I could only see the first couple strides before he disappeared into the woods – long, confident, powerful. And then he was gone.

I wrapped my arms around myself and kept staring at the woods for several minutes. There was a new apex predator out there now, a creature of unmatched strength and power. I could imagine everything fleeing in his path – deer, bears, mountain lions.

Everything but humans, whose senses wouldn't detect the threat the way animals did. I remembered that day long ago when he'd frightened the deer out of the woods, sending them running past me. They knew to get away from him. But people didn't.

And tonight, someone was going to become a meal. I shivered at the thought, even though I knew he'd do everything he could to leave his victim alive.

His victim. God.

I really needed to go inside and stop thinking about this, or else I was going to go chasing into the woods after him. And what? Stop him? As if I could. And even if I did, then what? He needed blood to survive. He needed to feed. I just had to trust that he'd stop in time, that he wouldn't kill.

I went into the lake house, set his necklace on the coffee table and built a fire, mostly to occupy myself. I put on some music. I cleaned the kitchen, which didn't really need cleaning. After that, I paced restlessly for a while. And then I looked at the clock. Only forty minutes had passed.

Christ.

Okay, so this was going to be incredibly difficult. Waiting, not knowing…not knowing if he was dead, or if someone else was.

After a while, in an effort to distract myself, I went and found my sketch pad and pencils, and tucked my feet under me on the sofa beside the fireplace. I hadn't done this in a while, and thought I'd be too worked up to do much now. But as soon as I flipped back the cover, I began to draw.

And of course, I drew Nikolai. He was all I could think about. I began sketching him from memory, swift strokes of graphite against paper.

Rose had done this too, I thought. She'd drawn him again and again, in her case channeling her unrequited love for him into creating pictures for herself, bits of him she could keep.

What I was doing was different. He and I were a couple. And yet, I had the same need Rose did, to draw him and…to do what exactly? To commit him to memory, in case I lost him? To record his overwhelming beauty, as if maybe distilling it to lines on paper would make it easier to come to grips with it? Or did I draw him in order to understand him?

He was a profound contradiction, kindness and gentleness and ethereal beauty wrapped up tightly, inexorably with a wild, deadly predator. Had Rose ever seen the dangerous side of him? Had she ever looked into his eyes and seen the vampire looking back at her? I didn't think so, because there was no sign of it in any of her drawings.

I looked at the sketch on my lap. This too was Rose's Nikolai –sweet, happy, kind. What would it take to transform the face on my drawing pad into the monster I'd caught glimpses of? How would I draw the predator? It was the same face, after all. The same man. The visible difference between the two was so subtle, just a slight shift in the intensity of his gaze, a sharpening somehow. The difference between looking at something and *watching*, maybe.

I could barely explain it and I certainly couldn't draw it. I didn't have enough skill to bring the predator's gaze to paper.

I turned to a new page and began drawing something else – the change in Nikolai's body language, right before he entered the forest. This was much easier. I could draw the way his body took on purpose, the way his hands flexed in some sort of anticipation. I imagined that body running through the forest, and drew four vertical rectangular panels, like a graphic novel: Nikolai darting through the trees, lithe, agile, so focused on the hunt that he didn't even notice the thorns and branches that tore at his skin.

Again I turned the page and drew four more vertical panels, and sketched Nikolai's vampire plunging deeper into the forest, running faster, faster…until he froze suddenly. Sensing his prey.

I couldn't make myself draw that, couldn't draw the person that Nikolai would come across, couldn't draw the fear in their eyes until he compelled them and made them compliant. I couldn't draw his hand on their skin, holding them down, a moment before he struck.

But I could imagine it, and it was vivid and terrifying. And just a little bit arousing.

"Christ," I murmured, tossing the drawing pad aside and scrubbing my palms over my face. Really? I was getting turned on by this? By the idea of my sweet, gentle Nicky, turning into a monster, a hunter, a predator?

He didn't want to be this thing. In many ways, he was as much a victim as those that became a meal. He'd been turned into this creature against his will, and now he lived as a slave to its needs. It was wrong to find anything erotic in what was happening tonight, somewhere out in those woods.

It was wrong to wish with a sharp, painful ache that it was *me* he was hunting. Me he would drink from. It was sure as hell wrong to feel jealousy toward the person he'd find somewhere in the night, the person that would feed him.

Damn it.

I launched myself off the couch and into the kitchen. This line of thought was going to drive me insane. I pulled open the cabinet and grabbed the last of the Jack Daniels. There was little more than an inch left, and I discarded the lid and drained the bottle's contents. It probably wouldn't be enough. I really should have anticipated my need to get smashed tonight and laid in a supply of hard liquor. Well, now I knew for next time.

Next time.

Shit.

This was going to happen again. And again, and again. As long as I was with Nikolai, there would be countless nights just like this. Nights I waited at home while he went out to get what he needed from someone else.

That thought made me pause. Yes, that was part of what was so hard about this. What he was doing wasn't sexual. But it did kind of feel like he was cheating on me, in an insane, convoluted, totally off the mark kind of way. Some part of my brain thought he should only be feeding from me, that it was way too intimate to do with anyone else.

"But that's crazy, because then I would die," I murmured. Maybe not the first time. Maybe not even the second. But he had an ongoing need for blood, it was all that sustained him. And how the hell did I think my body would be able to give him as much as he needed? Even if he held back and didn't rip my throat out, the cumulative blood loss from repeated feedings would kill me just as certainly.

I sat down on the kitchen floor and wrapped my arms around my knees. *It'll be the urge to fuck that sends him after you, far more than the urge to feed.* Nikolai had said that, in explaining why he had to get far away from me tonight. In explaining why his monster would come after me.

There *was* something sexual in what he was doing. It aroused him. Well, not *him,* but his monster, I told myself. But what was the point in making that distinction? They were one and the same. Then I remembered the spike of heat and desire that had shot through me when he bit me during sex. Christ.

I curled up on the kitchen floor, trying to detect even the slightest buzz from the liquor. Being a perpetual college student had really raised my tolerance to alcohol, I thought distractedly.

Man, tonight was going to fucking suck.

*****

Against all odds, apparently I'd actually managed to fall asleep for a while. I sat up on the hard kitchen floor and looked at the clock on the stove, which read 2:13 a.m. I hadn't managed to sleep the whole night away, but the fact that I'd slept at all was pretty remarkable.

My head was pounding. I got up only as far as my knees and reached a bottle of aspirin that was in the top drawer, then used my hand as a cup and scooped tap water into my mouth to wash down a couple pills. I started to lay back down on the floor, but my back and shoulders were so stiff from sleeping there that I forced myself to my feet and pointed myself at the couch. I turned off all the lights on the way into the living room, the complete darkness far more soothing to my throbbing headache.

I curled up in a ball on the couch and shut my eyes. And the skin on the back of my neck prickled. I opened my eyes again and lay perfectly still, my subconscious warning me not to move so I'd remain hidden, because it sensed some kind of danger.

Something caught my eye then. Movement. Something out in the night. I remained motionless, scanning the darkness beyond the windows as fear trickled like ice water down my spine. It was probably nothing, I told myself. A deer maybe. Or a raccoon. Something harmless.

Movement again, barely visible in the faint light from the sliver of moon. Something out past the deck. Out at the water's edge. Something big.

Something pacing.

I couldn't tell if it was human. Or Nikolai. It shouldn't be. He should be many, many miles away right now.

Wasn't he?

My throat had gone dry and it was difficult to swallow, the sound unbearably loud in the perfect quiet. I still didn't move, even though I knew that was pointless. If it was a vampire – mine, or perhaps another one – then it could see me perfectly right now in the darkness. It knew I was here. It knew I was defenseless.

What was it waiting for?

My heart was beating so hard that I wondered if whatever was out there could hear it. I sat up slowly, my hands sweating as I braced them against the couch. I wondered if I'd locked the front door, then almost rolled my eyes at my stupidity. The house was glass. If whatever was out there wanted in, it only had to smash a window. A lock wasn't going to stop it.

The thing in the dark stepped up onto the deck.

It was backlit and human in form, a bit hunched, broad shoulders outlined in moonlight, powerful arms ending in big hands that were contorted somehow. Curled like claws.

I had no idea if it was Nikolai.

It seemed to be breathing hard, its body expanding and contracting slightly as it drew air into its lungs.

And then it crouched slightly. Ready to pounce.

I vaulted over the back of the couch, fear a sharp taste in my mouth as I took the stairs three at a time. I had to get away. *Now*. I hurled myself across the dark bedroom, heading for the bathroom and the only solid walls in the house.

I didn't make it.

A hand closed around my ankle, and I slammed face down onto the wood floor. I hadn't heard glass shattering, I didn't know how it had reached me so quickly. But it had me now.

A heavy body leapt on top of me and I cried out as the air was forced from my lungs. Hands were tearing at my clothes, stripping me. I was brutally flipped over, and a mouth pressed against my own. It tasted of blood and salt. And it tasted of Nikolai. *Oh God, Nikolai.*

His tongue pushed into my mouth, and even as fear ricocheted through my body, I felt myself getting hard. Really? Even now, even when I was probably about to be ripped to shreds, I was getting an erection? Christ.

Nikolai pulled his jeans off, and his swollen cock pressed against my thigh. Again his mouth found mine, his kiss rough, demanding. Despite myself, I wrapped my arms around him and parted my lips.

He stood up and carried me to the bed and fell on top of me. And then he surprised me by reaching over and turning on the light. He was a mess, blood and dirt smeared over his face and body, matting his dark hair. His arms were bruised, his skin torn in dozens of places. "Nikolai?" I whispered. I looked into his eyes and saw only a predator looking back at me. Completely feral. Intense. Needing.

He kissed me again, hard, as a low growl rumbled in his throat. And then he bit me on the top of my shoulder, just as he'd done before. The growl deepened, and I heard him swallow.

Drinking from me aroused both of us, and he pushed his cock against mine. Any minute now, he'd mount me. He'd tear me open. I had no way to prepare myself. *Shit*. I pressed my eyes shut, my heart racing, my breath coming fast.

There was some sort of rattling sound, something getting knocked over, and then his hand wrapped around my cock. It was wet, kind of sticky. He worked my shaft, several long, rough strokes, before grabbing me by my shoulders. Nikolai flipped himself onto his back so I landed on top of him.

And he parted his legs for me.

I pushed myself up and stared at him, stunned. And then I glanced at my hard cock. It was slick with lube. When I looked into his face, only the monster looked back at me. Wild. Ferocious. But also full of intense longing. His lips parted slightly to reveal teeth that looked no different than usual, but that I knew could rip me apart effortlessly. He put his hands over his head and grabbed the headboard. As if chaining himself.

"Oh God," I moaned, and drove my cock into him, trying to control the force of my thrust, trying not to hurt him, even as my arousal made me wild for him. As I sunk into him he let out a bestial yell, parting his legs wider, rocking up to take me deeper.

Again and again I pounded into him, and when I was about to cum he let go of the headboard and grabbed me, holding me to his body. His fingers dug into my flesh, but I didn't care. I clutched him almost as tightly as he was holding me and came so hard that stars burst and swirled in my vision, his teeth tearing my shoulder again as his own climax shook him.

Finally I collapsed on top of him, aftershocks of that huge orgasm sending tremors through my body as I gasped for breath. After a minute I forced myself to unclench my hands, which were bruising his body, and pushed myself up to look at him. The pure, raw adoration in his eyes was the most beautiful thing I'd ever seen in my life.

Chapter Eighteen

When I awoke it was late morning. My body felt luxuriously sore. I lay face down on the mattress, enjoying the warm sunshine that fell across my bare skin.

Last night had been a revelation: astonishing, wonderful, dangerous. Mind-alteringly erotic. God, Nikolai. He'd been in his pure vampire form, wild and deadly. And he'd let me fuck him. No, more than *let me* – he'd *needed* me to fuck him. A tremor of pleasure shook me.

And afterwards, he'd just curled up in my arms and kissed me gently and fallen asleep, happy, sated. I grinned at that and rolled onto my back, stretching like a cat. Mmmm, definitely a good soreness. I wondered if Nikolai was sore, too. Probably.

Yet he'd still gotten up, and was probably downstairs making me breakfast. Sweet Nikolai, he really didn't need to do that. I rolled out of bed and padded downstairs to get him, but the kitchen and the ground floor were empty.

Maybe he'd gone home to change. He'd been a mess last night, and when I looked down at myself, I saw I was, too. Dirt and blood were smeared on my skin, my sweat having washed it off his body and onto mine. I needed a shower before I could even think about breakfast.

I went back upstairs and flung open the door, and jumped at the sight of Nikolai hunched in the far corner of the bathroom. "Nicky! What's wrong?"

Instead of answering, he drew himself deeper into the corner. His knees were pressed tightly to his chest, one arm curled over his head as if to shelter himself from something. He pulled his feet in tighter, trying to make himself as small as possible.

"Baby, can you tell me what's wrong?" I came up to him and crouched a couple feet away, looking him over, trying to see if he was injured. He was naked, his skin still streaked with dried blood and dirt, and some kind of red irritation bloomed over much of him, but I couldn't see what was causing him this much distress.

He looked at me, and I knew right away that he hadn't reverted out of his vampire form. His eyes were wild, but now instead of looking predatory, they looked absolutely terrified. "Nikolai," I tried again, "tell me what's wrong."

Instead of saying anything, he looked up. My gaze followed his, but all I saw was the bathroom: the tub and shower, the tile walls, the big windows set up high, the bright morning sunlight.

Which was threatening to ignite him.

"Oh God, Nicky!"

I leapt to my feet and looked around frantically. The entire room was bathed in light, coming in at every angle from the three large rectangular windows positioned about seven feet up in the high-ceilinged bathroom. Only a tiny triangle of the room remained in shadow, and that was the corner where Nikolai was trapped.

Quickly, I covered him with a big towel, but somehow I knew that wouldn't be enough. I ran into the bedroom and grabbed the heavy red blanket, and brought that to him as well, covering all of him. He drew himself more tightly into the corner. I guessed the blanket wasn't going to be enough, either.

I darted from the room again, trying to remember where his necklace was, the one thing that would keep him from burning. I looked around in wild desperation. Suddenly I remembered I'd brought it into the living room last night and hurtled down the stairs. It was on the coffee table, right where I'd left it.

I grabbed the necklace and ran with it to Nikolai and pulled the covers off his head.

"Here baby. Here," I stammered, my hands shaking as I tried to put the chain around his neck.

He cowered and pushed himself into the corner, and held a hand up to prevent me from putting the chain on him. In doing that, his hand passed into the light and he recoiled with a howl of pain and fear. "Nikolai, I have to get this on you. It's the only thing that stops you from burning!" I told him, but he wasn't listening. "Nikolai!" I yelled, trying to infuse as much strength into my voice as I possibly could. "I'm putting this chain on you, and you're going to let me!"

Nikolai stopped struggling and watched me for a long moment. Finally he sat up, just a little, and bowed his head forward slightly. Acquiescing. I dropped the chain over his head and he flinched when the cross settled against his chest. I told him, "Leave that on, no matter what. You're not to take it off. Do you understand?" He gave a single nod.

I stepped back a few feet, giving him some room. "It's okay now," I said softly, crouching down so we were at eye level. "You'll be safe from the sun as long as you keep that crucifix around your neck."

Slowly, carefully, he uncoiled his body, his eyes locked on mine. And then, in an act of pure trust, he crawled into the sunlight and came to kneel right in front of me, and leaned forward to rest his head on my shoulder. I took him in my arms and held him as his entire body shook. Even though he now knew he wouldn't burn, the sunlight still obviously upset him, so I said, "Do you know how to get to your home, Nicky, to the basement where you live?" Again he nodded.

"I want you to go there. You'll feel better in the dark, more secure than you feel here. Go there now and I'll join you in a few minutes."

He was gone before I could even register that he had moved. The front door clicked shut a second later. I exhaled and fell back onto the floor.

It was a couple minutes before I could move, slowly coming down off the adrenaline that had spiked in me when I'd found Nikolai at risk of burning to death, pinned down by sunlight. It had left me rattled and shaky.

But I had to make sure he was alright, that he'd gotten home safely. I got up from the floor and pulled on some clothes, then found a flashlight and headed into the forest. When I came to the clearing, I circled around to the hidden entrance and pried up the access to the basement, which was a lot heavier than I'd anticipated. I turned the flashlight on before I lowered the panel back into place behind me, and called out, "Nikolai, it's me." Which was stupid on many levels, not only because I didn't need to yell with his hearing, but because he could surely tell by my scent who I was.

He was curled up in a corner when I came into his room, hugging his knees to his chest. He was still naked and filthy, his eyes still wild in the sweep of my flashlight. I moved slowly and deliberately around his room, lighting just a couple of the oil lanterns. When I finished, I set the flashlight on his little nightstand and sat down on his bed. Nikolai hadn't moved. The predator in him was really accentuated in the dim light somehow, strong shadows defining his eye sockets and the hollows under his cheekbones.

I held a hand out to him and he rose slowly, his movements so sleek he seemed almost feline, covering the distance between us with minimal effort. Instead of taking my hand, he slid into my arms and we laid back onto the mattress.

When he spoke, it startled me. I hadn't even been sure he *could* talk when he was in this form. He said, "Thank you for helping me." His voice was deeper somehow. No, not deeper, I decided, just lacking the soft intonation that normally accompanied Nikolai's speech.

"I'm so sorry I forgot the necklace before I fell asleep."

"I forgot it too. Then when you brought it to me, I didn't even recognize it at first. I was so terrified of the sunlight that I couldn't even think."

"I know." I ran a hand over his tangled black hair.

After a pause he said, "I frightened you last night."

"Yeah, at first."

"I knew I wasn't supposed to come to you after I fed. But I needed you to fuck me." He ran his hand down my back.

"You were supposed to go a lot farther before you fed. It was supposed to take you a long time to get back to me."

"I found two hikers at a campsite only a couple hours into my journey. I was too hungry to pass them by."

"Did you kill them?"

"No."

"Well, good."

"Will you chain me and fuck me?" He asked it without emotion, a straightforward question.

"What, now?"

"Yes."

"You still want me to chain you? Even when you're...like this?"

"I bruised you last night and I had to struggle not to break you. If you chain me, I can just enjoy being fucked, instead of concentrating on not accidentally killing you." We were stomach-to-stomach in each other's arms, and he rubbed his cock against mine while he ran his tongue up my jugular vein. I was hard in a matter of seconds.

I rolled over him and out of bed, and quickly shucked my clothes. "Get on your hands and knees," I told him, my voice low. He complied instantly, his ass tantalizingly raised for me. I chained him quickly, shackling both wrists, then got on my knees behind him and worked his ass slowly and deeply with two lubed fingers as my other hand pumped his cock. A low growl rumbled in his throat, but it was a sound of arousal, not a threat.

He was back to being nonverbal now, moaning and growling in a way that made my cock throb. I slicked myself up and held onto his hips as I slid into him, and he pushed back onto me, impaling himself with a deep, satisfied sigh.

As I pumped into him I stroked his thick shaft, and he growled and tried to reach for me. The chains pulled him up short. So he tensed the muscles in his back and shoulders and jerked his hands back so violently, I was sure he'd shatter his wrists. "Stop!" I exclaimed, and impulsively slapped his ass.

His yell of pleasure was low, primal. He fought the chains, and again I brought my hand down on his ass as I thrust into him. "Stop, Nikolai! Before you break your wrists."

"Beat me," he growled, his voice gravelly as he panted hard. "Beat me and I'll stop pulling on the chains."

His raw desire spiked my own arousal, and I slapped his ass again and again as I fucked him. When I was about to cum, I grabbed his cock with my left hand, which stung from spanking him, and jerked him off roughly. We came within seconds of each other, yelling, bucking wildly, shooting deep into him.

Afterwards, we both collapsed onto our sides, my cock still in him, and I curled myself against his back. When I caught my breath I told him, "I kind of feel like I'm cheating on you, with you. I think you're wonderful like this, dangerous and wild. And I think you're wonderful the other way, too. I don't know where the man ends and the monster begins, and I'm not sure I care."

*****

We fell asleep in his little bed, and by the time we woke up, Nikolai was totally back to his old self and pretty thoroughly freaked out about what had happened. I unchained him, grabbed some clean clothes and led him back to the lake house. He turned down my offer to join him in the shower, and stayed in there a long time while I went into the kitchen and made myself some toast for lunch.

"That's all you're eating?" Nikolai had appeared at the foot of the staircase, his wet hair dripping onto his black t-shirt.

"Yeah. I didn't really have the energy to do anything elaborate."

He came up to me and pulled aside the collar of my shirt. The shoulder where he'd bitten me was bruised, but the bite seemed to have healed already. He said, "It's because I drank too deeply from you when you were fucking me. I'm so sorry." He picked me up and carried me to the couch, where he tucked me in with a blanket. "Take another nap if you can," he told me, kissing my forehead. "While you do that, I'll make you some lunch."

"I'm fine, Nicky," I told him. "Being a little tired isn't grounds for a major culinary intervention."

He knelt down so he was eye to eye with me, and said softly, "I could have killed you last night." He brushed my hair back from my forehead. "I know it in no way makes up for endangering you like that, but I have a profound need to take care of you now."

"Okay. Take care of me all you want then."

I did nap a little, and after lunch Nikolai carried me upstairs and bathed me, gently, carefully. After that he changed the sheets and tucked us both in bed. As he lay beside me and studied me, he said, "It terrified me that he came for you right after he'd fed. I tried to stop him from coming inside the house. Then you ran, and that triggered his predatory instinct. For a few terrible seconds, I really didn't know if he was going to kill you."

"But what you did instead was submit to me. I really don't believe you'd ever hurt me."

"Fortunately, he still recognized you as his mate. I mean *I* did…I don't know why I talk about the vampire like he's a separate entity…."

"I wish you'd learn to trust yourself, both sides of you, Nikolai. The way I do."

"How can I?"

"Last night, you came to me at the worst possible time, totally blood-drunk, totally given over to your vampire side. And even then, you didn't hurt me. That should tell you something."

"Yes…that's true. I am surprised that he – *I* – was so docile with you. But it's just so hard to trust myself, given my past. There are so many reasons why you shouldn't trust me, either, so much you don't know about me that you really should."

"Like what?"

"I've told you a little about my history, I've mentioned that I was made to be a soldier. My maker was a very ambitious vampire who created his own army in order to change the course of history in his favor. He used us to attack his enemies at night, when they were at a disadvantage. A handful of us could take out a hundred targets easily, wipe out a whole battalion in a matter of minutes. When I was first turned, I was completely wild, lethal. My maker harnessed that, put it to work in his favor.

I didn't think, didn't feel. I just did as I was told, just like the rest of the vampires he commanded, because vampires obey their makers without question, especially when they're first turned. And that's all my life was, only obeying orders, and the hunt, and the kill. Nothing more."

"I can't even imagine it," I said. "I can't imagine you, like that."

"Can't you? You've seen my monster in his pure form, or as close as I come to that anymore. Is it really so hard to imagine him killing?"

"Yes."

"The thing is, my time as a soldier isn't even the worst of it, it's not what I really regret. Back then, when I was newly made, I was far more animal than human. I lost myself entirely when I was turned."

He continued, "I was with my maker for only a matter of months before he became such a threat that another vampire assassinated him, and I was completely inhuman all that time. Then I and my fellow soldiers were locked up underground in prison cells, just in case my maker's second in command ever needed his own army. And slowly I came back to myself over the next year, slowly remembered what it meant to be human."

He paused, then said quietly, "When I was a soldier, I did terrible things. But what devastates me even more is what I did later, once I was on my own after my jailer was killed. By then I knew better, I had regained my humanity. But at first, I killed every time I tried to feed. I didn't want to, but I'd just get lost to the bloodlust and couldn't stop drinking in time. I didn't even know how to compel, which meant that many of my victims fought me, and some died that way."

He bowed his head, pain deeply etched onto his features. "It took me months to teach myself to compel, to do what I'd seen my master do when he fed. It took longer to learn how to stop drinking before I killed." He took a deep breath, and said quietly, "There were a couple accidents even after I learned what I was doing. The last time I killed was in 1962. The time before that was in 1938. I remember them clearly, and all the others I killed when I was learning to feed. I'll carry that guilt forever. I *want* to carry it, because it keeps me careful. I don't want anyone else to die because of me."

Nikolai looked at me as he said, "I'm so sorry. I should have told you all of this sooner, Nathaniel. I didn't want you to know the truth about me because I'm so profoundly ashamed of it, not that that's any excuse for not telling you. I'm the most selfish creature on earth to have ever gone near you, knowing what I am, knowing what I'm capable of."

I drew him into my arms, and he whispered, "How can you stand touching me? You know all of it now, you know that calling myself a monster is no exaggeration. You have to hate me."

"I could never hate you," I said. "You already told me you'd killed, I came to grips with that a long time ago. Knowing the details doesn't change anything."

"Even after all I just told you, you still want to be with me?" he asked incredulously.

I took his chin in my hand and tilted his face up so I could look into his eyes. "Of course. I want you like I've never wanted anything in my life, Nikolai. I want us to be together. Nothing can change that." I kissed him gently.

"I want that too." He was quiet for a while before saying, "I don't know what's going to happen when you have to go home to southern California. I can't follow you into a heavily populated area. I'd never be able to hunt without getting caught, and I wouldn't trust myself around all those people."

"We're going to figure it out, Nikolai. I promise you that."

Chapter Nineteen

"I want to try something new," I told Nikolai one morning after we'd been making out for a while, running my hands down his arms. "Will you let me?" A couple weeks had passed since he'd come to me after he'd fed. Day by day, he was learning to trust himself around me, slowly coming to believe he was in control of his vampire side. It was a work in progress, but I thought we were ready for what I had in mind.

He nodded, and I pushed the pillows and blankets off the mattress and instructed him to lay on his back, arms and legs forming an X. Quickly, I chained his wrists and ankles to the heavy bed frame. His thick cock stood tantalizingly at attention.

"You'll never be able to fuck me in this position," he told me.

I smiled at him. "I know."

"Then what are you going to do?"

"Something I hope you find incredibly pleasurable."

I ran my palm down his shaft, then took him in my mouth and sucked him until he was achingly hard. Then I picked up the little jar of lube from the nightstand and slicked up his cock, stroking him firmly. He moaned and thrust into my hand.

He seemed surprised when I slowed my strokes and then let go of him, and watched me closely as I picked up the lube again and scooped a big dollop of it onto two fingers. And then his eyes went wide as I reached behind myself and worked my fingers into my hole. "What are you doing?"

"I think you know," I said with a wink.

I spent some time working my opening with my fingers while slowly stroking his cock with my other hand. I was fairly impatient though, so pretty soon I was straddling his body, his cock pressed against my entrance. "Oh God, Nathaniel, are you sure?" He looked equal parts aroused and alarmed.

"Oh, I'm sure. What about you, do you want to do this?"

"Yes. God yes! But I don't want to hurt you," he said.

"You won't. I'll be controlling how fast and how deep I take you. I want you in me so damn bad." I lowered myself so my opening pressed against him. The fit seemed impossible. He was long and thick, far bigger than anything I'd taken inside me in my very limited experience.

But then my body opened just enough to admit the tip of his cock. "Oh God, Nikolai," I moaned, and slid carefully down him, just another inch. I held still to let my body get used to the size of him, and beneath me the predator flared to life in Nikolai's eyes. He swung his hands around and grabbed onto his chains, every muscle in his arms, chest and shoulders tense, perfectly defined. He didn't pull to try to get free, though. He was bracing himself, trying to force himself not to thrust into me.

My progress was frustratingly slow, but inch by inch I took him inside me. And when maybe half his length was in me I began to ride him, carefully at first. He threw his head back and yelled, then locked eyes with me and allowed himself to buck very slightly beneath me.

"Yes," I moaned, and soon I was taking him harder and faster, deeper into my body, as more of me opened up to him.

Soon we were locked in a primal rhythm, driving myself onto him, meeting his upward thrusts, my ass slamming against his body as I took all of his length in me again and again. I grabbed my hard, precum-slicked cock and began jerking off roughly as I rode him.

"Oh God! Nathaniel, I'm going to cum."

"Yes! Fuck yes, cum in me," I ground out as I rode him violently, driving him into my body over and over, jerking my own cock so hard it should have hurt.

He thrust up into me, and I felt the incredible sensation of his cum shooting deep inside me as he yelled, arching his back. "You're so fucking beautiful," I said as I rode him and milked his cock into me.

And then I was cumming too, shooting over his chest, a few drops reaching his lips as his tongue darted out to catch it. I dropped onto him and ran my tongue over his chest, then met his lips in a deep kiss, feeding myself to him. He moaned loudly and sucked my tongue, still thrusting into me even as the last of his orgasm ebbed.

"More. Please," he rasped. I leaned down and licked the rest of the cum from his chest, and again he sucked my tongue, wanting every drop.

I unlocked the chains and wrapped my arms around him, and he held me tightly as he said, "That was absolutely amazing. Thank you."

I grinned at him. "I was hoping you'd like it."

"I can't believe you did that for me."

"There's nothing I wouldn't do for you, Nicky," I told him, snuggling against his chest.

"I'm glad you didn't tell me ahead of time what you were doing. I would have been too afraid of losing control to go through with it if I'd known."

"Yeah, that's why I went for the sneak attack." I ran my finger along his lower lip, and he nipped my finger playfully. That reminded me of something, and I said, "I have a random question for you. Aren't you supposed to have fangs?"

"I used to," he said. "But my master filed them down – the man that kept me as a slave and brought me to America."

"Why?"

"It was a way to assert his domination over me, to render me helpless. He thought it would make me dependent on him, that it would mean I couldn't feed on my own, that I could only eat what he brought me. Needless to say, he was wrong. The rest of my teeth are perfectly capable of opening a vein."

"He was a monster."

"Yes. But still, I'm grateful to him," he said. "If he hadn't taken a liking to me, I would have died in that Russian prison. He got me out right before the whole place was to be destroyed by fire, our troops finally deemed unnecessary and sentenced to execution. I would have died there like all the other prisoners, never having gotten to experience the miracle of you."

"I'm no miracle." I burrowed my face into the little hollow between his shoulder and neck and said softly, "And really, when it comes right down to it, you deserve so much better than me. You're so far out of my league, Nikolai. It's actually crazy that someone as beautiful as you would even look twice at someone like me."

"You're kidding, right?"

"No. It's a simple fact."

"You really think that somehow it's *you* that's not good enough for *me*? Are you crazy?"

"I'm nothing special, Nicky. Maybe you haven't been around enough people to realize it, but there is absolutely nothing remarkable about me. Whereas you, in addition to being heart-stoppingly, stunningly gorgeous, are also fascinating and kind and intelligent and a million other good things."

Nikolai stared at me long and hard. Then he startled me by jumping out of bed and throwing me over his shoulder. He marched me into the bathroom and stood me up in front of the full-length mirror on one wall, holding me to him with one hand, while with the other he took my chin and turned my face toward my own reflection. "I want you to take a good look at yourself, Nathaniel," he said, his voice low, "and then I want you to explain to me how the fuck you could possibly think you're nothing special."

I tried to pull my chin out of his hand, looking at his reflection over my shoulder instead of my own. "Stop it, Nikolai. I already know what I look like. This isn't going to make your point for you."

"Just look, Nathaniel. Really look." He said that softly, releasing my chin and gently sliding his hand around my neck, resting his fingertips against my pulse.

I sighed and rolled my eyes, then did as he asked. I almost didn't recognize the person looking back at me. My hair was longer and blonder than usual and my body was tan (all over) and more muscular than it had ever been. But the real change, the significant one, was the fact that I looked happy. I murmured, "I look different, and that's because of you. You make me happy. Usually." I knit my eyebrows at him in the mirror but grinned too as I said, "When you're not trying to force me to look at myself."

He kissed the side of my head. "You're absolutely gorgeous, and so full of life and energy, it just radiates from you. You're like the sun, that warm, that vital. But you're more than just beautiful. You're also fun and incredibly talented and kind and charming and sexy as hell and so much more."

I just couldn't take compliments, I'd never been able to. I blushed and ducked my head and tried to deflect his words by saying clumsily, "You hate sunlight, it's deadly to you. Saying I'm like the sun isn't a good thing."

"It *is* absolutely deadly to me," he said, running his palm down my stomach, coming to rest just an inch above my cock. "But I still crave it with every part of me, even knowing it could kill me. You're just the same, just as beautiful and deadly. And I'm Icarus, overcome by your radiance."

"You have that completely backwards," I told him and then drew in a breath as his big hand swept the length of my cock.

He kissed my shoulder, his voice low and seductive as he said, "I don't." He ran his tongue up my neck, watching my reaction in the mirror.

I wasn't following the conversation very closely any more, arousal rising in me as I arched my back and rubbed my ass against his cock. But I still felt the need to correct his obviously flawed logic. "It's not me that's deadly. Your analogy doesn't hold up."

"But you are," he said, running one hand over my nipples while his other arm wrapped around my waist. "You're absolutely deadly. You call to me with every part of you." He pulled me against him and pressed his hard cock against my ass for emphasis, and continued, his voice growing rough, "You're pure, irresistible temptation. And every time I give in to you, every time I fly too close to the sun, that could be the time that ends me."

He bared his teeth and scraped them across my shoulder, and I gasped and flung my hands forward to brace myself on either side of the mirror as a wave of desire made my legs go weak. He said, "Because Nathaniel, if this is it, if this is the moment I finally go too far, the moment I finally kill you…" he pushed his hips forward, his cock right at my hole, and with a firm thrust, he was inside me. I gasped with surprise and pleasure. "If this is it, baby," he said as he began thrusting into me, grabbing my body, pulling me back onto him, "Then that's it for both of us. If you die, I do too. If I kill you, I kill myself in the very next moment." He was thrusting into me hard and fast now, my breath coming in quick little gasps. "I can't and won't live without you," he said, his eyes locked with mine in the mirror as he fucked me. He was pure vampire now. Unchained. Deadly. I didn't care. No, more than that: I *welcomed* it.

"Oh God, Nikolai," I moaned, locking my elbows to keep from being bashed against the mirror, thrusting my body back onto his cock.

In the voice of his monster, low, forceful, he told me, "We live together, and we die together. I don't want to kill you. I don't. But look how easy it would be right now. You didn't try to stop this. You didn't chain me."

"No, I didn't."

"Why not?" He drove into me, hard. "Are you letting me fuck you like this because you want to die?"

I pushed back onto his cock and moaned, "No. I'm letting you fuck me like this because I want to live."

"Oh God, Nathaniel," he ground out, lifting me up off my feet, arms around me as he bounced me on his hard cock. And then he was cumming in me, long hard thrusts sending his seed deep into my body as I yelled with pleasure and threw my head back onto his shoulder.

Nikolai kept going until he was thoroughly spent, then carefully eased me off his cock and lifted me in his arms. I was moaning incoherently and had no idea what he was doing, until I felt the wetness of his mouth close around my achingly hard cock. "Oh God, yes!" I yelled as he held me to his lips, taking me down his throat. And then I was cumming violently, without warning, my whole body convulsing as I cried out. He just kept sucking me, riding out my orgasm until I was drained, my body limp in his strong arms.

He pulled me into a hug then, and I clung to him while my body trembled from the aftershocks of that shattering orgasm. He carried me over to the tub and held me on his lap as he sat on the rim and turned on the water. I couldn't speak, couldn't even open my eyes.

After a while he shut the water off and lowered both of us into the hot bath. I lay against him like a rag doll, my body aching all over. But it was a wonderful ache, the feeling of being well-fucked.

He said quietly, "Explain that statement to me. *I'm letting you fuck me like this because I want to live.* We keep playing Russian roulette, we keep gambling with your life and mine. How is that living?"

I scooped up his hand and pressed it to my still-racing heart. "I didn't feel alive before I met you, Nikolai. I just existed, I went through the motions but didn't really *live*." I sat up and looked at him as I said, "You brought me to life.

I don't know, maybe the fact that you're dangerous adds to it. If some part of me thinks every moment might be my last, then I'm damn well going to enjoy that moment, every sensation, every emotion, every nuance.

"Or maybe," I said, brushing his hair back from his face, "the danger has absolutely nothing to do with it. Maybe it's just you, and it's us. Maybe it's the joy of having found you that makes me feel so totally alive. I don't know, exactly. But I do know that feeling's amplified when one of us is inside the other."

Nikolai thought about this for a while as I settled back onto his chest. He ran his hands down my back and over the curve of my ass, cupping it before sliding further down my thighs. And then his hands slid all the way back up to my shoulders again, and he hugged me and said, "Okay. I get it."

I rolled my head back slightly and looked up at him. "Yeah?"

He nodded. "I'm still going to worry about the danger I pose to you. But I guess I understand why this is also life-affirming." He pulled me to him, his hands tangled in my hair, and kissed me deeply before saying, "And it's the same for me, you know. I was just existing before I met you. Every day was like the one before it, quiet, lonely, never changing. I don't know how I survived it. Now that I have this to compare it to, I could never go back to that half-life."

Chapter Twenty

To beat the mid-July heat I'd spent a lot of the day in the lake, swimming lap after lap. I was trying to tire myself out, because I wanted to be able to sleep tonight. And that wasn't going to be easy, because Nikolai was going to go out and hunt.

It would only be the second time he'd hunted since we'd been together. For over a month he'd been subsisting on deer, elk, whatever he could find. It kept him alive, but I could see how it weakened him, too. His always pale complexion looked slightly grey, his body subtly leaner, his eyes just a bit stressed and underscored with blue shadows.

He'd been putting this off because he still didn't trust himself around me after feeding, still wasn't sure what he was capable of when consumed by bloodlust. The fact that he hadn't been able to stop himself from coming to me last time he fed, coupled with the fact that he'd chased me when I ran, had terrified him.

Aside from the stress of this hunting trip, life at the lake house had been wonderful. Our days were juxtaposed with the tranquil peace of just being together, talking, reading, drawing, cooking, and then fucking wildly, passionately, shattering the stillness with our moans and yells of pleasure.

Visits every other Friday from Bill and Chad helped mark the passage of time. Nikolai disappeared during these visits, though I told him he really didn't have to. They brought regular updates from my family and mail from my little brother Ryan, who'd been inspired by my comic books to draw his own. He sent me huge stacks of these, and I was delighted at his pictures and his attempts at writing phonetically. I sent outgoing mail back with the housekeeper in return, mostly funny little drawings for my baby brother and notes to my family assuring them I was not only still alive, but thriving.

I missed Ryan. I'd see him in a few weeks, when I was going to have to leave here. While I might have been able to convince my family to let me stay an extra month or two, I did eventually have to return to the rest of my life. The plan in sending me to the lake house hadn't been that I would stay forever, of course, only that I take some time to figure out my life, who I was and what I wanted.

In my time here, I *had* reached a couple conclusions. First and foremost, I knew I wanted my future to include Nikolai. And I knew I wanted to study art. Nothing had ever fulfilled me the way drawing did, and I wasn't going to give up on that so easily. When I went back to southern California, I'd need to find a full-time job, so I could afford an apartment for Nikolai and me. But I still wanted to figure out a way to fit some art classes in.

There were a lot of details to work out. But first we just needed to get through tonight.

At sunset, Nikolai was pacing nervously back and forth on the deck. He was dressed in a long-sleeved black t-shirt and black jeans: he was going fully clothed this time, and with his crucifix talisman in place around his neck. He turned to me when I came out to him and said, "Maybe I shouldn't go."

"You have to, Nikolai, you know that as well as I do. You need to eat." Yes, I could refer to it simply as eating, the idea of feeding from another person kind of compartmentalized away in my mind.

"I know I do."

"It'll be fine, Nicky. You'll see."

He let out a ragged breath and nodded, then ran his hands through his dark hair. He didn't move, though.

"Where will you go?" I asked.

"North, into Oregon, because it's less crowded. This time of year, it's really difficult to hunt. All the hiking trails and campgrounds are full of people on summer vacation. I'll have to find a remote location, maybe a back country trail."

I drew him into my arms and kissed him, and we held each other for a long time. Finally he took a deep breath and stepped back from me. "See you soon, Nathaniel."

"Be safe, Nikolai."

He nodded and walked to the edge of the forest. But he didn't transform himself like last time, he didn't look like a predator when he went into the woods. He just looked like a man, and a tired, hungry one at that.

I went inside and prepared to wait.

Chapter Twenty-One

Two days later, I was still waiting.

Dread settled cold and heavy inside me. Each passing hour became more agonizing than the last. Something was wrong. He should have been back by now.

Something had happened to him.

The morning of the third day, I knew I couldn't wait around any longer. There was no reason he should be gone this long. I had to find him, even though I didn't have the first clue how to do that. I emptied my backpack and reloaded it with a few supplies: a first aid kit, matches, bottles of water, a knife and a flashlight, and as much nonperishable food as would fit in the pack.

I didn't know how I expected to find him somewhere out in the back country, where he most likely was. I had no survival skills. Hell, I'd never even been hiking. This was going to be absolutely impossible. And yet, I had to try.

I drove down the long dirt road and onto Highway One north, then headed into Oregon. I was worried and scared and already exhausted, barely having slept since he'd gone missing. But

I was something else, too: I was absolutely determined to find Nikolai.

At a ranger station just over the Oregon border, I stopped and picked up a stack of free maps. I tried to sound confident as I asked the ranger to direct me to some hiking trails. "I want to go someplace remote," I said, "someplace in the back country, without a lot of people around."

The ranger eyed me appraisingly. He was only a little older than me, but big and solid and muscular, the kind of guy that had probably been a football player in high school. He was kind though as he said, "If you're just starting out and doing a solo hike, you may want to begin with something safer, a trail with more people around."

"I'm not a novice," I lied. "I've just never hiked in Oregon before, so I don't know the routes."

He remained skeptical, and said, "It can still be dangerous, hiking alone in an unknown environment."

An idea occurred to me then. "You may have a point. I heard some hikers got attacked a couple days ago. Can you show me where that was? I should probably stay away from that trail." I was totally bluffing, reasoning that if something had gone wrong when Nikolai had tried to feed, maybe that had generated a call for help from his intended victim.

And then, I got lucky. Really, really lucky. The ranger was all too happy to tell me about an incident that had happened two nights ago. He obviously hoped the story would dissuade me from trying the more remote trails, greenhorn that I was.

"A pair of hikers tangled with some kind of animal, probably a bear. It could have been worse," the ranger said. "They escaped with only mild lacerations because a third hiker caught up with them at their campsite and he carried a handgun. The animal rushed the third man, but he got a couple shots off and it fled into the woods."

"Did they get a look at whatever attacked them?"

"No, it was too dark to see very well. The third hiker, the one with the gun, just described it as a big, dark shape running at him, which kind of has to be a bear. The first two, they couldn't describe what it was or what had happened to them. I guess they were traumatized or something."

Or compelled, I thought.

The ranger added, "It's not like that happens all the time. But still, it's just another reason why you should stay out of the back country if you're hiking alone and don't know this environment."

I pretended to take his words to heart, and had him circle on a map exactly where the attack had occurred, so I could 'be sure to avoid that area.' Before I left the ranger station, I assured him I would stick to the more popular hiking trails, and wouldn't do anything that would necessitate a statewide search and rescue effort.

And then I went speeding off toward either a crazed bear, or maybe, just maybe, my vampire boyfriend.

Chapter Twenty-Two

I had been combing the mountains for three days. My socks were soaked with blood, blisters long since giving way to raw flesh. It had rained, so I was cold and damp. My food was gone. And I'd started drinking creek water when my supply ran out, something even *I* knew was wrong. But I wasn't giving up. I just knew that Nikolai was out here somewhere, and I was going to find him. It didn't matter that I was in excruciating pain. It didn't matter that I was exhausted. I dug deep, deeper than I'd ever thought possible, and just kept going.

I'd devised a systematic approach to searching the forest, a grid originating at the campsite where the alleged animal attack had occurred. The spot was easy enough to find…if you considered a ten hour hike easy. The hikers had cleared out quickly after the attack, leaving a fire pit and a couple items behind, and the bullet casings were right there in the dirt. I couldn't guess the direction the probably-not-a-bear had run off in, so I just started at the campsite and kept expanding the grid outward, pushing deeper and deeper into the woods.

With my knife, I marked the trees. I made up a code and set out rocks and sticks to indicate places I'd already searched so I wouldn't go in circles. I tried to be as meticulous as possible, not only to make sure I covered all of this area, but because if I managed to get turned around out here, I might never be able to find my way back out.

I thought about Nikolai constantly. If he really was in these woods, then by now he'd been out here several days. Did vampires die of exposure? Did they die of gunshot wounds? When I found him, I was really going to have to ask for some basic vampire physiology lessons.

It was close to nightfall on my third full day searching. Soon I'd have to stop for the night. I was just going to curl up on the ground wherever I was when the sun went down, and sleep right there. But a few weak, golden rays still filtered through the tree branches, so for now I pushed on. I wearily hoisted my backpack further up onto my shoulders. And then something caught my eye.

It was just a subtle reflection, weakly cast in the fading sunlight. Just the littlest glint of something, over to my right. I stepped around some rocks and bushes.

And there he was.

Nikolai's body was splayed out like a child in sleep, one arm across his chest, the other thrown to the side. His crucifix hung from his neck, draped over his right arm. That was what had caught the light.

He wasn't moving.

I whispered, "You can't be dead. You just can't be, Nicky." I approached slowly, fear making my scalp and my hands tingle, and knelt beside him. There was nothing, no sign of life. I pulled the knife from my pocket and drew it across one of my fingers, which I put into his mouth. And I waited, shaking with fear and adrenaline.

Then I decided that wasn't enough, and pulled my finger out and cut my arm, deep enough to get the blood flowing, but not so deep that I'd be dead from blood loss in five minutes. I pried his mouth open and pressed the cut to his lips.

Again I waited.

"You're not dead," I told him. "No way are you dead. I just found you, and now I'm *not* going to lose you."

It was getting dark, so I pulled the flashlight from my pack with my free hand and shone the beam over Nikolai. There was a hole in his t-shirt, near his heart. From a bullet, maybe? I used my knife to slice open his t-shirt and pulled away the fabric, still keeping my right arm pressed to his lips. There was a lot of dried blood on his chest, but no sign of a bullet wound.

I went to pull my arm away from his mouth to check that the blood was still flowing. Just then, his hands shot up and grabbed hold of my arm so tightly, I was sure the bones would snap. I was so startled that I cried out and pulled back instinctively.

That was when he lunged at me.

His teeth ripped into the side of my throat, and I cried out again. He was like a wild animal as he pressed me to the ground with his body, one hand around my throat to hold me still. He was drinking from me deeply, I knew, because with every pull I felt a little weaker, a little more light-headed.

I panicked and tried to struggle, but I was absolutely no match for him. He held me down effortlessly. My voice was rough and faint with his hand around my throat as I rasped, "Nicky. Nikolai, it's me. It's Nate."

I didn't even know if he heard me, and I was about to pass out at any moment. I tried one more time, my voice a whisper. "Nikolai, it's Nathaniel. Stop. You're about to kill me."

My field of vision was narrowing. I was drifting in and out of consciousness, my eyelids getting heavy. I was only vaguely aware of the pain at my throat ceasing, of the weight on my body lifting. Nikolai's face appeared, inches above my own. The light was faint, but I could see terror and recognition in his eyes. And blood on his lips.

I had to tell him something…something important. My mind was clouded, and I was so tired. I was going to let myself fall asleep, but there was something I needed to do first. Something I had to say. And then I remembered what it was, and whispered, "I love you, Nikolai. Don't kill yourself. You didn't know what you were doing. Please."

A warm, comfortable peace enveloped me then, and I let my eyes close. I'd done what I'd needed to. I'd found Nikolai. He was alive. And I'd said what I needed to say. I could let go now.

Chapter Twenty-Three

Consciousness filtered back in bits and pieces. Opening my eyes was a huge effort. Darkness was all around me. Shapes were moving in the dark, flying past quickly. I couldn't make them out. I was so tired, and I let my eyes slide shut again.

There was a pleasant scent right beside me. So familiar. "Nicky," I murmured.

"Oh God, Nathaniel."

Wasn't there something I was supposed to say to him? I thought for a while. I was being rocked…no, I was being carried. And we were moving quickly through woods. Woods….

Then I remembered what I wanted to say. "Nicky, don't kill yourself. Please. You didn't mean to hurt me."

He pressed his lips to my forehead, then said, "Just stay alive. Don't worry about me. Please just stay alive."

"I love you, Nikolai. I was afraid to say it before, but I'm not afraid anymore."

"I love you too, Nathaniel, more than anything." He shifted me in his arms, and in the next moment I felt him press something to my lips. His voice was urgent when he said, "Here, baby. Drink. I didn't give you nearly enough earlier. Please drink from me."

Already the rich, lush taste of his blood was filling my mouth, and I swallowed automatically. Warmth and energy spread through my body. Nikolai staggered, just for a moment. But he tightened his grip on me and kept going.

I was considerably more coherent now, and gently took hold of his wrist and removed it from my mouth as I said, "Nicky, put me down. I can walk."

"No, baby. You need to save your strength, you need to heal."

"So do you."

"I'll be fine."

"Is there a bullet lodged somewhere inside of you?"

"No, it passed all the way through me. But it tore a hole in my heart and I guess I bled out before the wounds healed. How long was I in the woods?"

"I think…I think it was six days."

"I can't believe you found me."

"I got lucky."

"You could have died, Nathaniel. And I don't just mean because I could have killed you, though I almost did. You could have gotten lost, injured, died of exposure, or countless other catastrophes. Promise me you'll never do anything like that again."

"Uh, no. I'm not going to promise that. If you don't come home, I'm damn well going to come and find you."

He sighed and then asked, "Were you drinking unfiltered water? Don't you know you're not supposed to do that?"

"How did you know?"

"The taste of your blood was off, because you were starting to get sick. My blood will help combat that and everything else you did to yourself, along with what I did to you," he said. "But I'm serious when I say you must never come after me again, Nathaniel. You really put yourself in jeopardy, especially by approaching a weakened, starving vampire."

"Let's argue about this later, when I have the energy to tell you there's no fucking way I'll ever leave you to die."

He emerged out of the tree line then, and murmured, "Thank God." My jeep was parked a few yards away. He'd covered the ten-hour hike in a fraction of the time.

Nikolai opened the passenger door and laid me gently on the seat, then reclined it back for me. He tossed my backpack in the Jeep, then rummaged around in the clutter of my car, and finally produced half a bottle of water and an energy bar for me, which I ate in two bites. I peeled my bloody shoes and socks off and sighed with relief, and he brought an old beach towel from the back and covered me with it.

"I think we should spend the night here," he said. "Hopefully you'll feel stronger after a little sleep, and then you can drive us home. I don't actually know how to drive, otherwise I'd do it."

He came around to the driver's side and slid behind the wheel, then reclined his seat back and curled up on his side facing me, arms wrapped tightly around himself. It was hard to see him in the dark, but his body language clearly showed his tension.

"You're still hungry, aren't you?" I asked quietly.

"Yes."

"Are you afraid you're going to hurt me?"

"No. If I was worried about that, I wouldn't be in here with you. The horror of suddenly regaining awareness in the midst of killing you is seared into me forever, and that's one hell of an appetite suppressant."

I reached out and caressed his arm. "Nicky, sweetheart, it really is okay now. We're both okay."

"Nathaniel, I'm so sorry. God I'm sorry. You shouldn't be with me. I don't deserve you." I leaned over and clutched him to me as he said, "I almost killed you. Another few seconds—"

"You didn't do it. You stopped yourself. Even as starved and disoriented as you were, you still stopped yourself in time." I held him tightly.

"I don't know how you can bear to touch me," he whispered. "I don't know why you're not afraid of me, after what I did to you."

Instead of answering that, I said, "Please don't leave me Nikolai, even if you think it's for my own good. I know the risks involved in being with you, and I accept them all."

"How did you know I was thinking about that?"

"Because I know you. You'd think you were doing me a favor, but you'd be taking my heart and soul with you when you left. Making the decision to keep us apart would destroy me more completely than anything you fear will happen if you stay."

He ran his hand down my cheek and kissed me gently. "I love you, Nathaniel, and I want you to be happy."

"Then stay with me forever."

Chapter Twenty-Four

I felt a lot better when I awoke, stronger and almost giddy with relief that we were both alive and together. It had been a miracle that I'd found him, and yes, a miracle that he hadn't killed me. We'd survived that. We could survive anything.

But Nikolai looked haunted, pain and regret clouding his pale eyes. He barely spoke as we began the long drive home. After about an hour, I stopped and bought a coffee and a couple energy bars at a gas station convenience store. Nikolai was hunched in the passenger seat, the hood of my jacket pulled up over his hair. He looked wild, nervous. He was terribly hungry after losing so much blood, and was watching everyone that walked past the Jeep the way a falcon watches a rodent.

I walked up to his side of the Jeep and gestured to roll the window down, and told him in a low voice, "You don't have to limit your feeding to the woods, you know. As long as you're someplace private enough, you could feed here, in this town."

"Are you insane?"

"You can't walk into the convenience store and snack on everyone in there, obviously, but what about the restroom around back? There are no security cameras in there, and people generally come in one at a time. I could keep watch outside the door, make sure you have the time you need to drink. You could do it to several people if you wanted to, just taking a little from each so they don't feel the effects."

He was staring at me as if I'd just suggested he burn the gas station to the ground. "You can't be serious."

"I am."

"And what do you propose to do with me once I'm blood-drunk and in full monster mode?"

"I intend to order you back to the Jeep, if you don't return there on your own."

"And if that doesn't work?"

"Why wouldn't it? Your vampire listens to me."

"It's a huge gamble. Here, in broad daylight, with so many people around...." I could tell he was considering it, though.

"Yeah. But you need to eat, and soon. You really think you're going to be up to returning to the woods tonight?"

"That would be…extremely difficult. But I can't involve you in this. What if I get caught? What if I lose control? What if—"

"What if it works?"

He watched me for a long moment, uncertainty in his aquamarine eyes. Finally he said, "Okay, but not here. We've already attracted attention by sitting out here having this debate."

"Fair enough." I jogged back around to the driver's side and got behind the wheel.

As we drove down the highway, I said lightly, "When we get home, I'm going to teach you to drive."

"Why?"

"Because you should know how to do it. It might be useful for you. Plus, it might be fun."

"If you say so."

At the next gas station, I pulled the Jeep into a parking space on the far side of the building. "I'm going to go in and case the joint," I told him with a grin. Then I added, "Actually, I'm going to buy a candy bar as an excuse for parking here. I'll be back in a minute."

He was agitated when I returned and tossed a soda and a Snickers on the back seat. And he said, "Someone just went into the men's room. He's alone in there."

"So what are you waiting for?"

He pressed his eyes shut and took a deep breath, then got out of the vehicle.

It went just as we planned. Nikolai went in and did what he needed to do, and I stood watch outside. The door to this restroom swung open then, startling me. The man that had been in there with Nikolai looked calm, happy as he wandered back to his car. I wondered what ideas had been implanted in his mind to cover the fact that he'd just been someone's breakfast.

We did this twice more. Two more motorists went into the restroom, one by one, and came out looking peaceful. Then Nikolai came out too. He'd washed his hands and face, his black hair damp around the edges. We got back in the Jeep wordlessly and I pulled out onto the highway. After a while I said, "You seem pretty calm. I expected your monster to give me some trouble after feeding that deeply, but it's like he's not even here."

His voice was low as he told me, "I need you to throw me over the hood of this car and fuck me raw, fuck me so goddamn hard that I feel it for a week. I need you to claim my body, mark me, own me."

"Oh God." I glanced over at him. And then I saw it, the glint of the monster in his eyes.

"I'm serious."

"I know. And I'll be happy to fuck you, just as soon as we're home."

"No fucking way can I wait until we're home." His voice was dangerously low.

"Well, you're going to have to at least wait until we're out of this town." I glanced at him again and asked, "Does feeding always make you horny?"

"*You* always make me horny. Feeding slightly lowers my inhibitions."

"Slightly...."

He ran a fingertip along my inner thigh, up and down, the softest little caress, his hand slipping up under the leg of my shorts. With each pass, he went just a fraction of an inch higher. And higher. My cock hardened in anticipation.

His fingertip lightly grazed my balls and I gasped. My breath was coming quick and shallow now, and I whispered, "You're right. No fucking way can we make it home."

"Find someplace to pull over." His voice was low, seductive, his touch surprisingly gentle as he traced a little circle on my balls through the thin fabric of my boxers.

I looked around in desperation, my cock throbbing, straining against its confines. We were travelling along the coast and it was the height of summer, so every turn-out was full of cars and people. Nikolai withdrew his hand a few inches, and then slid it back up my leg, this time inside my boxers. He couldn't reach much with my clothes in the way, but again he traced a light circle on my balls, this time right on my skin.

It was the smallest contact, but it sent a shock of pleasure and desire through me, making me buck my hips and moan his name. His fingertip travelled back down and then slowly up my inner thigh and I gasped. Then I murmured, "Nicky, you have to stop doing that. I'm going to crash the car." His response to that was to unbutton my shorts and slide down the zipper. Then he reached into my boxers and pulled out my throbbing cock. "Oh God. Nikolai, I mean it. I'm going to crash."

"Then find someplace to pull over." His voice was so low, so sexy. He lightly ran his index finger over my tip and came away with a glistening drop of precum. I glanced at him, and he met my gaze as he put the tip of his finger in his mouth and sucked off my juice.

I threw my head back and moaned, then took a wild left turn off the highway. I had no idea where I was going, but figured there would be fewer cars to crash into once I got off the main road. Nikolai meanwhile leaned over to me and hooked his thumbs in both sides of my boxers, and said, "Raise up for me."

I did as he asked, bracing my feet and raising my butt off the seat a couple inches. He pulled my shorts and underwear down to mid-thigh, my cock jutting up against my stomach. The feel of the seat against my bare ass was surprisingly erotic.

Nikolai growled again and lowered his dark head into my lap as I stammered, "Nicky, no. I won't be able to stand it. I'm still trying to drive. I—" I forgot what I was saying as his mouth closed around my cock and I cried out.

We were travelling into the hills, away from the ocean. Signs told me we were heading for a campground, which of course was going to be crowded in July. I tried to think, tried to focus as Nikolai sucked me. I was about to pull over right here on the side of the road and let him finish me off, to hell with the passing motorists.

But then I spotted a little access road to my right with a sign that said *Authorized Vehicles Only*. Normally I was so law-abiding that that sign would have stopped me, but right now I was too horny to give a damn, and I swerved the Jeep to the right. I wound a few hundred yards up the narrow, bumpy road and pulled into a little turn-out, then glanced around quickly, saw we were completely isolated, and shut off the engine.

Nikolai released my cock from his mouth and sat up and looked around, then turned to me and grinned. He was his monster, completely feral. Completely dangerous. I wanted him more than I'd ever wanted anything in my life.

He tore his clothes from his body and climbed on top of me, reaching down and flipping the lever beside my seat to drop it flat. His knees were on either side of me on the seat, and he took hold of my cock and positioned it at his opening. "Nicky," I gasped, "No. It's gonna hurt. You need more — ahhhhhh!" He lowered himself onto my cock, using only his saliva as lubricant. He didn't stop until I bottomed out inside of him and he was sitting on my hips, completely impaled.

He threw his head back and let out a low moan, almost a purr, and remained motionless on top of me for one long moment as a tremor undulated through his body. Then he tipped forward and met my eyes, hands braced on the seat as he began to ride me.

It was hard and fast and violent as he slammed himself onto me again and again, my fingers digging roughly into his ass as I pulled him onto me. We never once broke eye contact, locked together body and soul, as I thrust wildly up into him and he slammed down onto me. He knew I was going to cum a moment before I did, and clamped his big hand down over my mouth, leaning forward so his face was just inches from mine.

And then I was cumming and yelling, my cries muffled by his hand as I gripped his ass even harder and slammed him onto me and shot deep inside him. He bit his lip, hard enough to draw blood as he too came, obviously struggling to be quiet, shooting all over my stomach and my t-shirt as he rode me and I continued to buck into him.

He kept riding me until I was spent, and only then did he remove his hand from my mouth and kiss me gently before laying carefully on top of me. I was trembling violently, my body still dealing with the aftershocks of that mind-blowing orgasm. It was a minute before I could speak, and finally I said, "That was intense."

His laugh rumbled through his chest, and he pulled back slightly to look at me. "You could say that." I leaned forward and licked his bloodied bottom lip, and he grinned at that. "I like it when you taste me."

"Same here. Actually, I'm surprised you didn't bite me in the middle of all that."

"I wouldn't let myself, not after almost killing you in the woods."

"You know," I said, "back there in the woods really was the absolute worst case scenario. You were completely gone, completely consumed by bloodlust, and you still managed to stop before you killed me. If you can do that, if you can stop even when you're completely starving, completely depleted, then you really do have control of your vampire side." He didn't say anything, but I could see he was mulling that over.

A shrill sound in the distance caught my attention and I sat up quickly, bringing Nikolai up with me. I was still inside him, our arms wrapped around each other, and I asked, "What was that?"

"Laughter. There's a campground and a dozen people just on the other side of that tree line." His eyes sparkled mischievously.

I stared at him. "You knew that? And you still let us do this here?" I gave him a little push. "For God's sake, get dressed before we get caught!"

He chuckled as he pulled himself off my cock and landed in his seat in one fluid movement. He pulled on his pants and my hoodie while I yanked my shorts and underwear back in place and zipped up as he said, "We weren't going to get caught. I knew exactly where everyone was the entire time."

"So that's why you didn't let me yell," I said, pushing my hair out of my eyes and turning to look at him.

"Exactly."

I grinned a little, despite myself, and flipped my seat upright before turning the key in the ignition. As I swung the car around in an awkward six-point turn I asked, "So, do you feel better?"

"If you're asking whether I'm still hungry, I'm not. I drank enough back in town. That gas station restroom was a terrible idea, by the way. I'm shocked we didn't get caught." His big hand landed on my right thigh and he massaged it gently. "If you're asking whether I'm still horny," I glanced at him and he grinned wickedly as he said, "Drive fast."

My cock, seemingly oblivious to the violent orgasm I'd had just minutes before, stirred to life, and I licked my lips in anticipation. Nikolai watched my mouth closely, a sexy little growl escaping him. And he said, "I can smell it, you know, the moment you become aroused. It makes me want to do such bad things to you." He ran the edge of his thumbnail up the top of my thigh.

"Damn," I murmured, then swallowed hard, my throat dry. He grinned and reached behind me and grabbed the soda I'd bought earlier, unscrewed the lid, and handed me the bottle. "Thanks," I said before drinking half of it. "Do you sense it when I'm thirsty, too?"

"I *hear* it when you're thirsty, by the way you swallow." His hand returned to my thigh. "I hear it when you're hungry, too, way before you hear your own stomach rumble. I hear exactly how fast your heart is beating at all times, and if I really listen, I can hear the blood flowing through your veins. I also see you far more clearly than you could possibly realize."

He ran his palm up my thigh. "For example, I know there are fourteen freckles across your nose. They were much fainter before you started spending so much time in the sun. There are eight distinct shades of green that comprise your eye color. And thirty-eight individual shades of blonde and brown and red that make up your hair color, though that keeps changing, again because of your time in the sun." He glanced over at me. "Shall I go on?"

"Yes."

"You have nine scars on your body bigger than a quarter inch. And I'd very much like to know how you got each and every one of them."

"Not sure I could tell you. Anything else?"

"You injured your right leg once. There are no visible signs of that injury, but you favor it very slightly, especially when you run."

"I didn't realize I favor it."

"I know."

"I tore the ligaments in my knee during high school, when I was on the track team. I thought it had healed completely." I glanced over at him. "How can you possibly know so much about me?"

"I'm just telling you what I've been able to observe."

"So you're actually able to count individual strands of my hair," I said disbelievingly.

"Yes."

"What else?"

He closed his eyes, then said with a little grin, "You have eleven moles on your body.

Would you like me to recite each of their locations without looking?"

"There's no way you can do that," I told him.

"My favorite," he said smugly, eyes still closed, "Is that tiny one on the inside of your right wrist. If you look really closely, you'll see it's almost a perfect heart."

I came to the stop sign at the highway, and held my right wrist in front of my face. There was a tiny mole there, which I'd never noticed before. It was miniscule, and I really had to squint at it to see that it was, in fact, heart-shaped.

"There are two on your left bicep," he continued. "They're three-quarters of an inch apart, and nearly identical." One glance confirmed he was right. "And one here." He picked up his hand from my thigh, and leaned over and tapped the side of my left knee. Right on a little mole. "There are three on your back," he continued, "One on your left shoulder blade and two on your lower back. The remaining four," he said, opening his eyes and grinning at me, "I'll show you with my tongue when I have you naked."

I stared at him in dumbfounded amazement. "How did you do that?"

He just shrugged, and gently brushed my hair back from my eyes. "I told you, I see you more clearly than you realize."

"That's not just *seeing* me. You've memorized me."

"You do the same thing. I've seen your drawings of me, the ones you do on your own when I'm not around. You draw me precisely."

"Yeah, but that's different."

"Only because you don't have vampire sight or hearing. You draw me exactly as you see me. The human eye can't pick out the different shades of brown and black in my hair, or the slight nuances in my eye color. It's impossible."

I was still at the stop sign and still staring at him. "Okay. But I guess the most perplexing part is why you would bother. You can't help but see the moles and freckles and scars, but why do you catalogue them? I don't get why you'd bother learning these things about me, why they'd matter enough to you...."

"Nathaniel, *I love you.* You're fascinating to me, and I want to know absolutely everything there is to know about you. From the big things to the very smallest, like how many freckles are on that cute little nose."

I threw the car in park and grabbed his face with both hands, kissing him deeply. Then I told him, "I can't even tell you how much it means to me. I was so used to feeling invisible, always unnoticed. I just…I don't even know what to do with this much love and attention."

He smiled at me and said softly, "If you let me, I'll spend the rest of your life making sure you feel cherished."

That was such a huge statement. And the fact that he said the rest of *your* life was notable too, because his life would, of course, go on for centuries after I'd been and gone. He'd watch me grow old, wither away, while he remained exactly like this. I tried to imagine it, me at eighty, stooped and wrinkled, and him every bit as radiant as he was now. I tilted my head and looked at him. Great for me, right? I'd get a hot boyfriend forever. But he'd end up stuck with Yoda.

He frowned slightly, watching my expression closely (and now I knew exactly *how* closely). "Did I say something wrong?"

"You don't want to end up with Yoda," I told him.

A short burst of laughter escaped him. "I wasn't aware that was an option."

A thought occurred to me, and I veered from the subject by asking, "Do you actually know who that is?"

"Of course."

"When did you ever see Star Wars? Or any other movie, for that matter?"

"I love movies. I used to watch them at a drive in theater on the coast. I'd sit on a hillside behind the theater, so I was apart from people. I saw hundreds of movies that way, until it finally closed down just a few years ago."

"You watched without sound?"

"I could hear the speakers perfectly, even from a couple miles away," he told me. "It was pretty much the only time I ever let myself get close to civilization. And even then, I wasn't all that close."

I put the car back in gear and turned onto the highway as I told him, "Okay. So, you know what I mean when I refer to Yoda: the fact that I'm going to get all old and wrinkled, and you're going to remain exactly the same. What are you going to do with me when I'm eighty?"

"God, I hope you make it to eighty. I hope you make it to twenty-three, which is challenging, since you're spending all your time with a vampire."

"Really, though," I said, applying the accelerator and passing a big RV. "You're not going to want me then."

"Are you kidding? Why wouldn't I want you, if by some wonderful miracle you made it into your senior years?" Nikolai was staring at me incredulously.

"Would you ever think about changing me, to make me like you?" I asked the question idly, just out of curiosity more than anything.

He swore vividly in Greek, crossing his arms over his chest. And then he growled, "You're kidding, right?"

"I'm not saying you *should*, or that I want you to. I just wonder if you've considered it."

"Why the hell would I consider that? Why would I condemn the love of my life to an eternity of darkness and misery? So that you, too, can live with the horror and the torment of being a monster? I don't think so."

"Okay. I just was curious." I glanced at him. His brows were knit, his arms wrapped tightly around his chest. "Is it really that bad?"

"Worse."

"I'm sorry, Nicky. I didn't mean to upset you."

"What's most upsetting is the fact that you somehow think I wouldn't want you when you get older."

"Not just older. *Old*. Bald. Saggy. Wrinkled. Maybe you can't picture it, but I sure as hell can, and let me tell you: it's not gonna be pretty. You think my freckles are cute? How cute are liver spots?"

Nikolai sighed and said, "You'll still be *you*, Nathaniel. You'll still be the man I love. And I would be so fucking thrilled if you actually made it to old age that I would look at every line and wrinkle as an absolute triumph."

I rolled my eyes, but kept silent.

Eventually, he uncoiled himself a bit and returned his hand to my thigh, and I rested my hand on top of his. I grinned and said, "I think it's cute that you swear in Greek."

He grinned a little too. "That's all that remains of my life as a human prior to being turned. It's kind of a shame."

*****

Eventually we pulled up to the lake house. It was so good to be back here. I led Nikolai by the hand inside and up the stairs, and stripped him and then myself as the shower warmed up. We washed each other thoroughly, days worth of dirt and blood and sweat running down the drain.

We climbed into bed after that, both of us pretty thoroughly exhausted. I snuggled against him and ran my hand over his bare chest. There was no sign of injury now that all the blood had washed away, and I murmured, "I can't believe that being shot through the heart didn't kill you."

"I can't die from a gunshot. Fire, beheading, or a wooden stake through the heart are the only things that can kill me. But losing that much blood when I was shot left me completely helpless. If you hadn't found me, I'd never have been able to feed myself and recover."

I glanced up at him. "You mean the movies actually got that right? Wooden stakes, and all that?"

"There's some truth behind a lot of the vampire stories."

"Go figure."

He ran his fingertips up my arm as he said, "I got to learn all about vampire lore and culture when I was locked up after my maker's death. The prison was full of others like me. Some had been vampires far, far longer than I had been. They'd talk, tell stories, pass on bits and pieces of our history. There was nothing to do *but* talk. At least at first. But after a few years, they stopped feeding us, and one by one all the voices fell silent as one vampire after another went dormant."

He shifted slightly, pulling me closer to him. And he said, "I'm grateful for those few years when we were being fed. Several of the warriors were Greek, but there were many other nationalities as well. Over time, we learned each other's languages, shared the histories of the places we'd come from, and even learned about the vampire culture we'd been reborn into. I wasn't able to tell them anything, since I hadn't retained what I'd known when I was human. But I learned so much from the others, and their companionship, even as faceless voices in the depths of that miserable prison, helped keep me sane."

Nikolai was quiet for a while, and then he said, "Even though I never wanted to be a vampire, during my time in prison I came to identify with the other men, the others like me. I realized I was part of a brotherhood, a family almost, and it was comforting to feel I belonged to something. I internalized some of the vampire culture and history, its rituals, customs. I think in part, I did this as a way of honoring the men that had fought at my side, the men that were slowly falling silent around me, and that would eventually die in that miserable, lonely prison." He paused again, then said softly, "I wish I could have saved them. I didn't find out until it was much too late that they'd all been killed, that the prison had been destroyed by fire. And by then, I was on another continent and under the control of a cruel master."

"You've been through so much, Nicky. I can't even imagine. It breaks my heart to think of what you had to endure."

"Don't let it upset you, baby. It was a long time ago. And really, I wouldn't change a minute of it."

"Why would you say that?"

"To rewrite any of my history would mean I never would have wound up here, in this place, at this time. I never would have met you. So everything I endured was worth it, because it ultimately brought me to you, Nathaniel."

Chapter Twenty-Five

Nikolai kissed me awake the next morning, and as he ran his tongue down my chest I smiled and murmured, "That is the best way possible to wake up."

"Sorry," he said between kisses across my belly. "I tried to let you sleep in. I really did."

"This is way better than sleep," I murmured, reaching down to stroke his dark hair. His tongue ran down my shaft and I gasped and added, "Way, *way* better."

"I want you to do something for me, Nathaniel," he said before taking my cock in his mouth and sucking it until it grew hard between his lips.

"God," I moaned. "Anything."

He released my cock and said, his voice low, "I want you to tie me up and fuck me."

"Absolutely. But do you really need to be tied up? We've had sex several times without using restraints and you didn't lose control."

"It's not that I need it," he said with a grin. "I just like it."

I smiled at that and rolled on top of him and kissed him long and hard before sitting up a bit and saying, "You know, yesterday some mention was made about bending you over the hood of the car. Wanna give it a whirl?"

"God yes," Nikolai murmured. He leapt out of bed and scooped me up in his arms, dropped keys and a container of lube in my hands, then grabbed some chains. He cleared the staircase in one leap as I laughed and held on tight, and brought me outdoors.

When he set me down, I pushed him against the front bumper of the old Jeep and kissed him passionately, then smiled and said, "Turn around, baby."

He grinned at me and bent over the hood, widening his stance so his ass was tantalizingly exposed. I snapped a cuff to his right wrist, then hooked the free cuff to another set of shackles, repeating that process until I had a daisy chain long enough to feed into the driver's side window, run across the dashboard, and pull back out the open passenger window. The cuff at the end of this chain got secured to his left wrist.

He was already hard, his cock leaking precum. I ran two fingertips up and down his shaft and over his swollen tip, getting them nice and slick, and spread him with my other hand.

Using his precum as lube, I pushed my fingers into his tight hole. He was totally aroused, his powerful muscles glistening with sweat in the July heat as he flexed his broad shoulders, bracing himself by wrapping his hands around the chains. Impulsively, I brought my free hand down hard on his ass and he moaned, "Fuck yes." I spanked him as I fingered him roughly, and he bucked his hips to drive himself onto my hand until we were both wild with desire.

I pulled my fingers out of him and quickly slicked my throbbing cock, and impaled him with one long, hard push. "God yes, fuck me Nathaniel," he rasped as I took him hard and fast, my body slapping against his, the Jeep rocking and creaking from the force of my thrusts. After just a few minutes of this I shot my load deep into his body, his yells of pleasure mingling with mine.

He still needed to cum, and I needed that to happen inside me. I pulled out of him and fumbled for the keys, and unlocked his wrists. He immediately figured out what I wanted, and jumped up on his back on the hood of the car, leaning against the windshield. I scooped up a big dollop of lube and climbed up on the hood with him, stroking his cock a couple times to get it nice and slippery.

I straddled him and positioned his tip at my hole, then took his cock to its base by sitting down on it. He moaned and began thrusting up into me as I rode him, holding on to my hips, bouncing me up and down on his hard shaft. I looked into his eyes, and yes, he was completely wild, completely lethal. So fucking sexy.

Soon he was cumming in me, big spurts filling me. I rode him to the end of his orgasm, then laid down on his chest, panting, my heart racing. He shifted me slightly, still inside me, and kissed me before touching my cheek and whispering, "God, you're beautiful."

I grinned at that, and instead of arguing as usual, I just said, "Thank you."

"Come on baby, I'll make you some breakfast," he said as he slid out of my body and picked me up.

As he carried me inside, I murmured, "How do you have the energy to move after that?"

He shot me a smile. "By being a vampire."

Nikolai put me on a stool at the breakfast bar, and turned on my MP3 player and swayed around the kitchen – almost dancing, that was a first – while feeding me blueberries and cooking me breakfast. And when he'd finished cooking, he scooped me up and carried me out to the deck, where he sat me on his lap and put the big plate of food in my hands.

"Just how many people are you feeding here?" I asked, looking at the mountain of food he'd heaped on my plate. But I demolished it all and then asked for seconds, which he provided with a huge smile, turning the music up when he was back in the kitchen.

After I'd eaten, I stood up and held a hand out to him, and said, "Dance with me, Nicky."

He stood too, smiling down at me, his pale eyes sparkling. "I don't know how to dance."

"Me neither. So we'll make it up as we go along." I drew him to me, one arm around his waist, his left hand clasped in mine, and we swayed to the music as he kissed me gently. I wrapped my arms around his neck, opening my mouth, his tongue caressing mine.

After a while he said, "I love how you've grown over these last few weeks, how you've found your courage and confidence."

"Have I?"

"Absolutely. Look at what you did to find me in the woods. You found such strength, such resolve within yourself. You kept going, day after day, trying to find me. You never gave up. That was incredibly courageous."

"I adore you, Nikolai. Of course I was never going to give up."

"Most people would have. But not you."

"Never. Not where you're involved."

"This feels so strong, so solid," he said softly after a while. "Like we're both sure of each other now."

"Exactly. I feel like we both trust not only each other, but ourselves."

He kissed my forehead and said, "I was so worried before, I was so scared of hurting you or killing you. You're right that what happened back there in the woods really was the absolute worst-case scenario. And if I was able to stop myself in that situation, then I really must have control of the vampire."

"Yeah, you really do."

"Somehow, since I've been with you, the line between him and me isn't so obvious anymore. That side of me used to be something I kept compartmentalized, locked away until I absolutely had to feed. But now, it doesn't really feel like something that's separate from me. And surprisingly, I actually like that. I feel more in control this way. More whole."

I brushed his hair back from his forehead and smiled at him. "I'm glad you're coming to terms with it."

"He still worries me. But the more I drag him out into the light, the more I'm learning to trust him…trust myself."

"That's wonderful, Nicky."

"I never want to be apart from you, Nathaniel. It scares me to think about moving into a more populated area, but because it's so unfamiliar, not because I fear killing anyone. I've learned that I'm much stronger than I realized, much better able to control myself. I feel like I can trust myself around people now. And the rest of it, getting used to a new environment, well, you'll be with me and you'll help me adjust."

"I will. I'll even teach you to drive, make you a proper city dweller," I said with a grin.

He laughed and said, "Now that's a scary thought."

"Nah. It'll be fun."

The song ended, and Nikolai swung onto the lounge chair with me on top of him. He traced his fingers up my bare arm and asked, "Have you thought about what you want to do after we leave here? I know you were supposed to be figuring out your life, your career. Do you have any answers?"

"I know I always want to be with you," I said with a smile. "That much I figured out. As far as a career, I decided to sign up for a couple drawing classes when we get back to southern California, probably at a community college. I'll need to find a full-time job so I can afford an apartment for us. But I can still take night classes and pursue a degree in art that way. In a few years maybe I can get a job doing illustration or graphic design or something along those lines."

"Do you want to move back to Long Beach?"

"No, it's too developed. You'd never be able to hunt. There are actually some fairly rural parts of southern California though, towns at the edge of all that urban sprawl. Someplace like that would be ideal, it'd be relatively uncrowded, but still close enough so I could visit my family regularly and commute into town to work."

"I'll figure out how to help with expenses," he said. "It doesn't all have to be your responsibility."

"What about your plans for the future, Nicky? We keep talking about what I want, but what do you want?"

"You."

I smiled and said, "You've got that already. You're going to have lots of opportunities once we move into a more populated area, chances to explore different interests. Do you think you might like to go to college, or something like that?"

He considered this for a while. "I never gave my future any thought. After having lived through so many centuries, I guess I just got in the habit of existing in the moment, not really looking ahead. And really, now that I *am* looking ahead, the only thing that matters to me is building a life with you."

"I want you forever, I want to be with you every day of my life. I love you so much." I kissed him again, then met his gaze and said, "Will you marry me, Nikolai?"

He gasped, lips parted, his eyes wide with surprise.

And then he said yes.

Epilogue

We were married the first week of September in Long Beach, California. The ceremony was a simple one. Nikolai and I both wore jeans and button-down shirts, and we got married on the beach in front of Irv's condo. My family attended, and my little brother Ryan was best man. He was so proud. And he made Nikolai a friendship bracelet as a welcome-to-the-family present, which Nikolai never took off.

I have to say, my family took it pretty well. I came back from Del Norte County with a beautiful boyfriend that I'd never mentioned and announced we were getting married the following week. They were stunned, of course, but then my mom said, "Well, why the hell not?" She'd accepted Irv's marriage proposal a few weeks after their first date, after all, so what could she say?

Beforehand, Nikolai went to the DMV and got a driver's license, to serve as his ID for our marriage ceremony. I'd been teaching him to drive for weeks, but the fact that he passed was sort of a miracle. And, okay, he had to compel the clerk at the DMV into thinking she'd verified his documentation, because of course he didn't have any, but he passed the test fair and square. The name he put on his license was Nikolai Logan. He actually took my last name, which was a wonderful surprise.

The part of our ceremony that my family wasn't a part of happened the night of our wedding. We'd gone through the human ritual of marrying, and that night we went through the ritual of sharing blood, according to centuries-old vampire custom. We both took turns offering our blood and our lives to one another, in an ultimate act of commitment.

Because my cash situation was on the nonexistent end of the financial spectrum, we then honeymooned for a week in the vacant apartment that my family used to live in. My mom hadn't been able to sublet it and was under a lease until the end of the year, so Irv had been paying the rent on it for her. It was a utilities-included unit, so we had hot water and electricity. We hung Rose's painting of the lake on the wall and pretended that was our view, slept on an air mattress, and spent our time either fucking like bunnies, or holding each other and kissing and talking for hours on end. It was an absolutely perfect honeymoon, as far as I was concerned.

And then my husband (husband!) shocked the hell out of me by handing me a brochure toward the end of our honeymoon and saying with a shy smile, "This is for you, Nathaniel.

I've enrolled you at this art school in Santa Barbara. That's my wedding gift to you."

I sat up on the air mattress and leaned against the wall. "What?"

"I should have asked you first, but I wanted to see your face when I surprised you with it." He was looking at me hopefully.

I stared at the piece of paper in my hand, totally stunned. It looked like a brochure for paradise. "This is amazing. But how? We don't have any money."

"We do, actually. Remember on Monday when it took me over an hour to get you some bagels? Well, I didn't actually get lost like I said. I went to Irv's office. Rose bought me a few stocks back in the 1920s and some of them survived the Great Depression. Irv helped me sell them." He grinned at me and said, "Rose thought the automobile was a pretty cool invention back then. Turns out buying shares in a few different car companies was a good call."

"You're kidding, right? You have to be kidding."

"No baby, I'm not. Irv's helping me sell an old pocket watch, too. Apparently it's gold and pretty valuable. Anyway, I'm not saying we're rich, but at least you won't have to struggle like you used to."

"So I can really do this?" I clutched the brochure in both hands, as if it was a mirage that might suddenly disappear.

"You start Monday."

"I can't believe you've been keeping all of this a secret. How did you stop yourself from mentioning any of it sooner?"

"I didn't want to get your hopes up until everything was certain. I had no idea if the stocks or the watch were worth anything, but it all worked out better than I could have hoped." He looked really pleased with himself.

"Thank you so much, Nicky!" I kissed him and then shook my head. "I can't believe this is happening. How could my life possibly be this perfect?"

Nikolai drew me into his arms and said softly, "You just married a vampire, love. Your life is far from perfect. I can just hear the lies you're going to have to spin when your family realizes your husband never ages. And every time I hunt, it's going to be stressful as hell for both of us. But," he added, "I'm also going to see to it that you're happy every single day, because that's what you deserve. I'm going to take care of you, just like you'll take care of me. My investments will see us through the next few years, and by then you'll have a wonderful career in the arts. I'm thinking I might go to school too, maybe figure out a career of my own."

I took his face between my hands and kissed him again before murmuring, "I love you so much, Nikolai."

"I love you too, Nathaniel," he said, then pulled back to look at me, his beautiful aquamarine eyes sparkling. "Now how much is it going to freak you out if I tell you about the other half of your wedding present?"

"Other half?" I echoed incredulously.

"We have an appointment tomorrow with a realtor. I want us to have a real home, one that's all ours. There's a little cottage in the hills outside Santa Barbara that I want you to see. It's nothing fancy and really tiny, but it's near the art school and fairly secluded, too."

My eyes had to be as big as saucers, my mouth hanging open. Finally I stammered, "You didn't have to do all of this for me, Nikolai, you didn't have to spend all your money. I only need you."

He took hold of my hand and kissed the simple silver ring on my left hand, the one that matched his, and said, "You've got me, baby. Forever."

I shook my head. "This has to be a dream. I'm going to wake up any minute."

He pulled me to him and kissed me, deeply, passionately. Then he asked, "Still think you're asleep?"

"Yes."

"I know how I can convince you you're awake." He pulled his t-shirt over his head and stretched out on the mattress, looking up at me with a big smile. "Come here, Nathaniel. Come claim your husband."

****

Thank you for reading!

For more by Alexa Land, please visit:

http://alexalandwrites.blogspot.com/

Made in the USA
San Bernardino, CA
13 December 2014